He'd caught

And Martin had

that to his advantage. He rolled the guy face down and twisted the man's left arm behind his back.

The attacker was disarmed and subdued, at least for a bit. Martin headed straight for Paige.

Another man in a ski mask was wrestling her into submission, despite her kicks and struggles. Martin felt a surge of protective energy rush through him. Just before he reached them, one of Paige's kicks connected, and the man reared back. Martin made use of the momentum, pushing the guy to the side. The man tumbled off Paige and onto the ground, and Martin fell near him, landing hard.

"Run!" he yelled.

She scrambled to her feet. But instead of heading in the direction of his car, she took off on the muddy footpath, into the darkness of the mountains.

Rebecca Hopewell is the kiss-only pen name for an award-winning romance author. In addition to writing, she loves to read, wander in the forest and talk with friends and family. A perfect day is when she manages to do all four of these things! Rebecca lives just outside San Francisco.

Books by Rebecca Hopewell

Love Inspired Suspense

Danger on the Peaks
Dangerous Mountain Threat

Love Inspired Mountain Rescue

High-Stakes Blizzard

Visit the Author Profile page at LoveInspired.com.

DANGEROUS MOUNTAIN THREAT

REBECCA HOPEWELL

Recycling programs for this product may not exist in your area.

ISBN-13: 978-1-335-95719-1

Dangerous Mountain Threat

For questions and comments about the quality of this book, please contact us at CustomerService@Harlequin.com.

® is a trademark of Harlequin Enterprises ULC.

Love Inspired
22 Adelaide St. West, 41st Floor
Toronto, Ontario M5H 4E3, Canada
www.LoveInspired.com

Printed in Lithuania

Ask, and it shall be given you; seek, and ye shall find;
knock, and it shall be opened unto you:
For every one that asketh receiveth.

—*Matthew* 7:7–8

To my son for bringing enthusiasm and
good conversation on our wilderness adventures.
Hopefully we'll never get stuck in a tent on a
mountain during a lightning storm again.

ONE

In the past two weeks, Paige Addison had listened to her twin sister's voicemail message enough times to memorize it. Yet as she came to a stop at the top of the muddy driveway of their grandmother's cabin, she couldn't help herself. She pushed play one more time.

"I'm following a story. I need to lie low for a few weeks. You know where to look if you need to reach me. Love you."

That was it. Following that, nothing. Even before the message, Layla had been mostly offline the last few weeks pursuing some newspaper investigation, and now Paige had precious few clues to figure out what was going on. She had the voicemail, the location of her sister's usual hideout—their grandmother's cabin—as well as the last-known site of her sister's cell phone, compliments of their location-sharing app.

Layla had been on the curve of the mountain road a little over a mile from the cabin when her cell service cut off, and she hadn't been back in range in three days. Very strange.

Paige had been in the middle of serving lunch to Esperanza, a widow who was recovering from knee surgery, when she'd let her sister's call go to voicemail. In her job as a home health care professional, personal calls were off-limits when she was with her patients, but maybe she should have bent the rules just once? Paige loved her job, especially the discussions with patients who had such interesting lives and stories. Talking seemed to stave off the loneliness she saw in too many clients' lives, and she loved the way she made a difference in their day, just by talking and listening.

Paige appreciated a quiet life. There was nothing she loved better than sitting by her apartment window with a mug of peppermint tea and a book in her lap, but she could admit that sometimes she got lonely, too. Sometimes she wished for something more. Nothing that changed her life dramatically, just a little change. She'd dated, most notably a firefighter that she really liked…until he was called off to battle an explosive fire season for months. Waaaay too stressful. She had local friends, but not the kind she was comfortable confessing worries to. Her closest friend was her sister.

Paige had gotten a handful of messages from Layla over the years about *lying low*, their code for a stay in the cabin while Layla finished an investigative piece for the *Sacramento Chronicle*. Sometimes Layla worked better without the temptation of the internet, and other times… Paige didn't like to think about those other times. Layla always waved off the danger, but just in case, Paige wasn't supposed to come near her sister while she was chasing a story. In fact, it was better if she also kept a low profile. As an investigative reporter, Layla had made more than a few enemies. But being an identical twin came with plenty of upsides, too, and one of them was that "twin sense" they both seemed to have. It was hard to explain to anyone who wasn't a twin except that when Layla was unhappy or in danger, Paige could somehow feel it.

This was exactly what was happening right now. Why she'd come to find Layla at the family cabin.

Please, Lord, keep my sister safe.

"Ready, Maggie?" Paige scratched her golden retriever behind the ears, and the dog sat up in the passenger seat, tail wagging.

The driveway to their grandmother's cabin was barely wide enough for Paige's forest green Jeep Cherokee. It curved through the trees and around a clump of garage-size granite boulders before ending at the cabin, right in the middle of a pine forest, just before the mountain took a steep decline. The good thing about the long driveway was that it insulated them from the noise of the two-lane road, allowing Paige and her sister to disappear, undisturbed, into their favorite corner of the Tahoe mountains. But the downside presented itself in front of her: the narrow driveway was next to impossible to navigate during the spring, when feet of snow melted into slushy puddles and the lane turned to mud. Back when her grandmother still lived here, they'd top it with gravel every few years, but clearly a few years had become too many. There was a fifty-fifty chance her car would get stuck if she started down the driveway slope. She needed to hike in.

Paige smoothed the fur on Maggie's head, and the dog gave her an enthusiastic lick. She opened the door and stepped out of the car, her hiking boots squishing into the soft forest floor.

"Come on, girl," she called, and Maggie jumped onto the driver's seat, then hopped down into the mud. The dog took off down the lane, splashing through a puddle, kicking up dirt as she sped down the familiar trail, oblivious to the more ominous reasons behind their visit. Paige followed, rounding the enormous granite boulders. As she came to the other side, she caught sight of an old red pickup truck. Layla's truck.

A burst of hope drove her forward. Maybe this was just one of the many times Paige had spent days worrying about her sister when the reality was much more banal. There was that time her sister had spent five days in the mountains, gathering sources about the impact of the new luxury Pinewood Resort on the older more rustic hotels in the area. Paige had been worried then, too, but Layla hadn't been under any threat other than an impending deadline. There was almost certainly a benign explanation for why her sister had been offline for the last three days. Maybe she was just hard at work? Still, Paige's gut was telling her different.

The driveway opened into a clearing. Originally, back when her grandparents built the place, the cabin had been surrounded by towering pines, but after forest fires tore through the area, ravaging houses and towns indiscriminately, they'd cleared a perimeter as protection. The upside was their new sunny perch gave a view of the sharp gray mountain peaks, still dotted with snow, and the deep green valley gave the place less of a lost-in-the-woods feel to it. This also meant Layla should be able to see her coming. Any minute, her sister would open the front door, run out and hug her. Any minute.

Maggie bounded up the front steps of the cabin as Paige approached the porch. The classic Tahoe A-frame was over fifty years old, and it looked its age. The weathered wood could use another coat of varnish, as could the hand-carved shutters, but the smaller A over the porch was still holding up, steep enough that the snow slid off the roof before it got too heavy. After a warm spring, the only snow left around the cabin was piled in slushy rows below the gutters. Paige climbed the familiar steps, but as she reached for the door handle, the last flickers of hope turned to wariness. The door was ajar.

An icicle of foreboding trickled down her spine.

"Layla?" she called.

Every instinct told her that something was off, but Maggie stood next to her, her head cocked, as if to ask, *What are we doing?* Normally, she'd keep the retriever outside until she'd cleaned her paws, but today wasn't a normal visit. Paige needed all the support she could get.

"Layla?" she called.

The wind shushed, traveling up the mountain through the pine branches just beyond where the cabin was perched, but from inside, there was only silence. The thick wooden door creaked as Paige pushed it open, and Maggie followed her inside. No barking. The dog always gave a few excited yips when she sensed another person, friend or stranger. As far as Maggie could tell, no one was there. So why did Paige have this sinking feeling that something was wrong?

The dog took off down the hall and into the living room, her claws scratching on the hardwood floor. She charged back to Paige seconds later with a ball in her mouth and dropped it between them. Her tail wagged as if to say, *Time to play!*

Paige was waiting for the tingle of fear down her spine to fade. She wanted it to disappear, this sense that something bad had happened, but it wasn't going away. Slowly, she stepped into the hallway, inspecting her surroundings. On the floor in front of her, there were traces of dried mud. The only reason Layla would wear boots in the house was the same reason Paige wore them right now: if something was wrong. The tracks forked at the end of the hall, one set into the kitchen and the other set into the living room. Maggie sprinted up and down the hallway, batting the tennis ball, then dropped it in front of Paige's feet again. Paige picked it up and threw it absently, then turned to the living room.

The pillows at the far end of the couch were squashed, as if someone had just gotten up, and on the dark wooden coffee table lay a half-full glass of water and a paperback about the Gold Rush. The scene was completely normal, as if Layla had stepped out of the room recently.

You know where to look if you need me.

Her sister's words from the voicemail ran through her mind again. Paige focused on the message. She'd been so worried about her sister's first sentence about lying low that she hadn't thought much about the second part. She'd just assumed Layla meant that she should go to the cabin. But what if her sister meant something more specific? Paige closed her eyes, pushing away the fear until... She opened them again, and her gaze darted to the fireplace mantle, loaded with three generations of family photos. She scanned pictures from weddings, family hikes and ugly Christmas sweater contests until her gaze rested on a small silver frame. It was the place she and Layla used to hide secret messages to each other in their favorite summer game, top-secret spy, during which they saved their grandmother from fake kidnapping scenarios. The hiding spot would mean little to anyone else but Paige.

Maggie was panting at Paige's feet with the ball in her mouth, but she ignored the dog and headed across the living room to the mantle. She lifted the silver frame, barely glancing at the picture of Layla and her, seven years old, with identical wispy brown braids, identical brown eyes and identical red-and-white-striped shirts. Paige flipped it over, feeling around for a note. But there was no note. Instead, taped to the back of the frame, she found a key.

She ripped off the key and turned it over in her hand. The

cold metal against her skin sent a shiver through her. It was long and completely flat, with the number 10–33 engraved on it. She knew exactly what this key unlocked—the family's safe deposit box at First Trust Bank in Clover Valley. In addition to general family valuables like the deed to the cabin and her grandmother's wedding ring, her sister used the box to store work material too sensitive to keep at home. If Layla had left the key for Paige, her sister was keeping something in there. She prayed it was somehow tied to Layla's disappearance. It was the only lead Paige had.

She carefully set the photograph back in its place and jogged down the hallway toward the front entrance. Maggie followed after her, the ball still in her mouth.

"We're going to leave this here, girl," she said, prying the ball from the dog's mouth and shutting it inside the cabin.

She and Maggie made her way back down the driveway and she loaded the dog in the car. She needed to get to town.

As she drove down the cabin turnoff and headed out onto the mountain road, Paige considered what she knew so far. Could Layla have been chasing a story and ran into trouble?

Being a certified nursing assistant didn't put Paige in nearly as much danger as Layla's job put her in. Of course, nursing wasn't as adventurous or ambitious as being an investigative reporter. Paige had always wanted a peaceful life, but she wanted to live close to her sister, too. After high school, when Layla attended Sacramento State for journalism, Paige had followed and started in a training program to be a home health care professional nearby. They'd both agreed to move back to their hometown, high in the Sierra Nevada, after college. But while Paige thrived in the quiet life of Clover Valley, her sister had chafed against the slower pace, so Layla had moved back to Sacramento for a job that had her chasing stories across the country.

Her parents were busy caring for her grandmother in New Mexico, and their attitude was that Layla always turned up…which had proven true so far. Still, this time felt different. Paige often wished that at least one of her close friends from high school—a group coined the Fabulous Five—would move back to Clover Valley. They knew Paige and Layla well. At least she could talk to them about her sister's radio silence and they would take her seriously.

Twenty minutes later, Paige pulled into the parking lot of First Trust Bank in the center of Clover Valley's Main Street. A cloud of fog had descended over the mountains, and the parking lot was as quiet as the sleepy town. It was low season, too late for skiing and too cold and muddy for the summer hiking and rafting crowds.

Paige wiped the remaining mud from Maggie's paws with a towel she kept in the Jeep, and they both climbed out of the truck. The sky had darkened, threatening rain, but it was impossible to tell when or how much through the mist. A lone black van was parked a block away near the urgent care center, and a white SUV and blue sedan were parked across the street in front of Hosey's Outdoor Adventure Sports. Hosey's—every time she passed it, she still thought of Martin, even though they'd only seen each other occasionally since she and Layla had moved to New Mexico their senior year. He had kept in better touch with Layla, and Paige tried not to think about that detail. He'd moved away to San Francisco for college and stayed, where his uncle's private investigator business thrived. It had been months since she'd let herself look at his social media posts, not since the last time she'd met up with him in Sacramento… Her face heated with embarrassment. She wasn't going to think about that right now.

Paige stomped her boots in front of the old stone building, then looked down at Maggie's darkened front paws. "We're kind of messy, girl. Let's hope Lorraine is working."

The thick glass door to the bank was heavy, and she pulled it open and entered the quiet grand interior. Paige scanned the tellers until she spotted her friend's familiar tortoiseshell glasses and dark curly hair. Good.

"Can I leave Maggie here?" she called, trying to keep the worry out of her voice.

"Of course," called Lorraine, but as Paige approached the teller booth, her friend gave her a searching look. "What's going on?"

"I need to look at our safe deposit box."

"I hope nothing serious has happened," she said as she took Paige's license from under the plexiglass and began the protocol.

"Everything is fine," said Paige quickly.

Lorraine was an old friend from high school, and though she meant no harm, she was chatty, and this was a small town. News traveled fast. If Layla was in danger, Paige had no idea where an accidental slip of the tongue could lead.

"We're all set." Lorraine grabbed the keys and led Paige through the locked door, back to the vault. The room was cold and quiet, and silver metal doors of different sizes with brass hinges lined every wall. Her friend stuck the master key into the 10–33 slot, and Paige did the same. She pulled out the long box and set it onto the wooden table in the middle of the room.

Lorraine gave her one more searching glance, then tucked a stray curl behind her ear. "Just let me know when you're done."

"I will."

With one last glance over her shoulder, Lorraine left

Paige alone in the safe. She took a deep breath and lifted the lid.

There was a stack of manila envelopes with titles like House Deed and Insurance Policy printed on them, and the jewelry boxes that lined one side were neatly stacked. But wedged on the side of the jewelry, Paige found a lumpy white envelope with the name Anushka Patel printed in all capital letters. It was Layla's writing, and Anushka was Layla's editor at the *Sacramento Chronicle*. Paige swallowed. Why had her sister left this envelope here and not given it directly to Anushka?

Paige picked up the envelope and turned it over. It was sealed. She pressed against the bulge in the middle of it, gently tracing the shape against the paper until she had a decent guess about what it was. A thumb drive. Paige was almost sure of it. A thumb drive for Layla's editor that almost certainly held a story she was working on. She stared at the silver doors that surrounded her, trying to piece this together. Most likely, the thumb drive held a part of the story. Maybe it was a backup of vital evidence? If the story was finished, Layla would have taken it directly to Anushka. There must be something her sister was still uncovering, something big. Something dangerous enough that she'd hide a copy of her evidence and be forced to lie low.

Paige's heart thumped harder in her chest. She leaned against the cold metal wall, then slowly sank to the floor, the weight of the past hour's revelations hitting her. Her sister had disappeared. Would Layla want her to go directly to Sacramento with the thumb drive and deliver it, or would she want Paige to find her? Past experiences suggested that as soon as the story came out, Layla's danger would dissolve. But that scenario assumed Layla had finished her investigation, and her phone message suggested otherwise. Paige needed to find Layla. Her sister was in trouble; she could feel it. Her heart pounded in her chest as questions flooded her. How could she help her sister? Where could she even start?

Guide me, Lord. She let the prayer flow through her, calming her thoughts.

"Just breathe," she whispered to herself. "You'll figure this out."

Whatever she was going to do, sitting here on the cold marble floor of the bank vault wasn't helping. Paige got to her feet and shoved the envelope into her purse. Maybe if she looked at the information on the thumb drive, she could figure out where to look? She called for Lorraine and together they locked the safe deposit box.

"Did you find what you needed?" asked Lorraine, giving her a searching look as they walked out of the vault.

Paige nodded, not trusting her voice. Her hands shook with fear and urgency as she headed for the front door. Maggie wagged her tail as she approached, and when Paige squatted next to her, Maggie nosed her hand, and her tail swished back and forth. Paige gave her a quick scratch on the head.

"We're going to figure this out, girl," she whispered, then stood. With one last wave to Lorraine, she pushed open the bank's heavy door.

It was drizzling, and the sidewalk was damp. As she reached for the hood of her black all-weather coat, Paige spotted a man across the foggy street walking out of Hosey's Outdoor Adventure Sports. Tall, broad shoulders, warm brown skin…it looked like Martin Hosey.

An uncomfortable mix of happiness and embarrassment made her stop, momentarily pushing aside the urgency of her fear. It had been months since the Fabulous Five reunion at a Gold Rush–themed restaurant in Old Sacramento. All five of them showed up, Martin from San Francisco, Juana from Orange County, Benji from San Diego and Layla from just outside Sacramento. Only Paige was in their hometown, as Benji had pointed out with a mix of admiration and confusion. Though they'd known each other growing up, they hadn't become close until they all signed up for junior ski patrol training at Alpine Resort. Something about the intensity of the training and the mix of personalities came together and they'd all clicked. How many times had the gang ordered pizza back at Martin's after ski practice or search and rescue training? His parents had even invited Layla and her over a handful of times when their own parents were away for weeks, caring for their grandmother, before they'd moved the family to New Mexico for good. While they had known each other for years, after that winter, the friends became inseparable…until Paige and Layla moved away just before senior year. It was never really the same after that.

Still, they'd kept in touch and tried to find a reason to get together at least once a year.

Last time was for Juana's birthday. Juana and Benji had driven up together from Southern California, and Paige had stayed the night on her sister's sofa. They were older now, but the long dinner that drew out into the night still glimmered with their teenage connection, at least for the most part.

Martin had been distant at the reunion dinner. It was hard to explain why she'd gotten that feeling since he had talked as much as anyone else. But it felt as if his heart hadn't quite been in it. And yet there had been moments when she'd met his gaze, and the connection between them flickered back to life. She'd invited him to dinner, just the two of them, a few weeks later. They'd spent hours talking about everything, from their families to their jobs to the best movies they'd seen lately. The whole evening had been so lovely, so easy, and as she'd watched Martin from across the table, she felt a spark of hope that something deeper was blossoming between them. Clearly he didn't feel the same, judging from the way he'd ghosted her afterward.

Paige squinted through the fog. Yes, that had to be Martin. Paige's face heated uncomfortably, but she lifted her hand in a tentative wave. The man tilted his head a little, then a smile spread across his face. It was Martin's smile, and it triggered memories of the dinner that crisp winter evening, sitting across from him, the votive candles lighting up his brown skin, brightening the dark depths of his eyes. As Paige opened her mouth to call out a greeting, the screech of car tires on pavement came from the nearest corner on her left. She whipped around just as a large black van roared to a stop in front of her. The side doors flung open, and two men jumped out. They were dressed head to toe in black, with hats pulled down low and neck warmers over their noses.

One of the men grabbed her arm, yanking her purse with his other hand. It all happened so quickly, and the air rushed out of her lungs as panic took over. All she could see was a strip of pale skin, dark eyebrows and blue eyes, narrowed with aggression. Maggie gave a yip of excitement, and she heard her name somewhere in the distance, pushing Paige back into action.

"No." She tried to pull away, but the man clawed his fingers into her arm, his nails scraping against her jacket.

The other man grabbed for her feet. She kicked but toppled off balance. She dropped to her knees, then pulled against the man's grip, making herself dead weight as she tried to pry her arm free. The man's hand slipped down the wet arm of her jacket, and she fought, batting at him, twisting, as Maggie jumped up on top of her, yapping at the men. The dog had never shown an ounce of aggression, but this man didn't know it.

"Get them, Maggie," she said.

Maggie crouched and let out a bark, like she was ready to play, but the man with her purse reared back, jerking it out of her hand. The contents spilled out, first the envelope with the thumb drive, then her wallet, her phone, tissues, lip balm, two overdue bills, all hitting the wet pavement. Paige lunged for the envelope, her knuckles scraping against the sidewalk as she fisted it. Maggie dove in beside her as the man scrambled to grab the bag. The other man grabbed her from behind, and her breath whooshed out of her. The dog nipped at the man's hand and let out a low growl, different than anything Paige had ever heard. The man behind her froze.

"We're attracting attention," said the guy in front of her uneasily.

Maggie's growl grew louder.

"We know where she is now. We'll come back for her," the other guy muttered. Then her arm was free. Her legs sprawled out under her. She was lying on the wet ground. The two men jumped back into the van and sped away. She drew in a shaky breath, frozen in place, processing the last moments, and it registered that her purse was gone, along with her wallet.

The screech of tires tore Martin's attention away from the woman on the road and he took in the large black van. It didn't have any notable markings. The plates were covered with mud, but he could see a bit of the word Nevada printed at the top of it before it hurdled around the corner and out of sight.

Paige—Martin was almost sure it was her. He had a very bad feeling about this.

"Hey! Paige?" he called. He started across the street, hurrying as he took in her prone figure on the roadside.

He hadn't seen much, only a flash of her coming out of the bank before the vehicle had driven up, blocking his view. From across the street, he thought he'd heard a dog's growling and low voices. It had happened so fast. Martin's gut twisted. *Harden your heart*, he told himself, the way he had countless times on investigation assignments that had led him down a path that exposed the darker side of humanity. That mantra, *harden your heart*, was the only way to think straight in these kinds of situations. Even if it felt as though hardening his heart had slowly chipped away at the good-natured optimism he'd once had. He'd had to leave San Francisco and come home to Clover Valley in search of that part of himself. But right now, he needed to put all that aside.

As Martin approached, a shudder ran through his body. It *was* Paige. Who was in the van? What had happened? *Focus.*

He heaved a shaky breath. For the second time, he froze. He'd never frozen up on a job before, but as he stared at her still body, it was as if all the movement had been sucked out of him. Was she badly injured?

Then she moved. Sat up.

"Maggie," she whispered as she reached for the dog and wrapped her arms around the animal's neck.

Pull yourself together.

But how could he harden his heart when one of his oldest friends might be hurt? Whatever had just happened, he had come a moment too late to help. That thought sent a tremor through him. He had to push this pain away. That was the only way to think straight in these situations. Why would someone try to pull Paige off the street? Martin took one last scan of their surroundings for any lingering signs of danger, then knelt beside her. She was shaking.

"Good girl," she whispered. "You're such a good girl."

Paige prodded at one paw, then the next, gently bending them. The dog didn't protest.

"Is she okay?" His voice came out rough from the emotions he was trying hard to suppress.

"Martin." It was just his name, but she said it like a prayer. Paige's eyes fluttered open, revealing the deep brown he remembered so well from years of junior ski patrol. "As far as I can tell, she's fine."

"Are *you* okay?"

His mind incongruously jumped to the way her eyes had sparkled across the candlelit table on that one night that left him vulnerable in all the ways he couldn't handle right now. His gut twisted again, and for the first time on this trip to Clover Valley, Martin could finally admit to himself how much he'd hoped to see Paige. Over the years, as he'd driven from San Francisco up into the Sierra Nevada, through the familiar rocky pass and into the pine forest where his hometown was nestled, he'd thought countless times, *Maybe this time I'll call Paige. Just to catch up.* Then, after the Fabulous Five meetup for Juana's birthday, she'd texted him. He'd felt a flutter of happiness at seeing the text, which had managed to break through the pessimism that had plagued him too often. He'd met her in Sacramento, halfway between their lives. Everything had been so lovely that night in ways he tried not to think about because he'd worked so hard to protect that raw territory she could so easily expose. He wasn't the same person as he was back in high school, especially after the investigation into his friend's brother had gone so terribly wrong. And if Paige heard about this investigation and the pessimism that followed, a pessimism that had taken over his thoughts all too often, he didn't want her to look at him with that same worried look his parents gave him. When she'd messaged him for a second dinner, he'd debated about how to answer. And debated some more. And when she called, he didn't answer, telling himself he'd call back when he could figure out how to explain what he was going through without making himself feel more raw, more vulnerable. It never happened. Months had passed since then, in which they hadn't spoken.

Still, he'd found himself hoping that if they ran into each other in Clover Valley, just in passing, maybe he'd figure out how to talk to her. Maybe he could keep up the veneer of his old self, pretend for a while, just to remember what it felt like to talk to her. But it had never happened, and little by little, he'd stopped thinking about it.

Yet right now, as Paige's gaze met his, the hope he'd tried to bury came back to life, flooding him with warmth. Except he needed to block that out. Focus.

"What just happened to you?" He couldn't forget the danger he'd just witnessed.

"I—I'm not sure. Those men tried to pull me into their van, but I dropped to the ground and kicked, and then Maggie scared them off. They jumped back into the van and left with my purse." She shook her head. "And my wallet..."

So close to terrible harm.

Martin pushed aside a wave of protective instinct that threatened to overwhelm him. Those feelings wouldn't help them right now. He needed to discern what happened and if she was still in danger.

"You fought them off." He wrapped an arm around her shoulder.

Paige gave him a little smile. "I had help."

He let Maggie sniff his free hand, then gave her soft wet coat a few strokes. "You are such a good girl," he said. He turned back to Paige. "Why would those men try to pull you into their van?" Between his glimpse at the perpetrators and the deep voices, Martin had deduced the two attackers were men.

"You have no idea who they were?"

"No. But I have a feeling they're after Layla."

Martin had been a private investigator long enough to understand that this scenario didn't look good. Even if these men were technically after Layla, they were careless enough to target her twin.

"It sounds like both you and your sister are in danger." Martin frowned. "Do you want to call and tell her what just happened?"

Paige shook her head slowly and opened her mouth to speak, then hesitated. Maggie turned and licked her on the neck, and she squeezed her dog.

"What is it?" he pressed gently.

"I have no idea where Layla is," she finally said. "That's why I was here at the bank. I found something that might help me find her."

Martin's private investigator radar was going off loudly, and he could feel the familiar drive coming to life, the drive to uncover whatever was behind this attack. That felt good, the logic kicking in, pushing away the emotions that had come rushing to the surface when he saw Paige hurt. Except this wasn't his job. He was supposed to be taking a much-needed vacation, the one his parents had pushed him to take. One that was supposed to remind him of the goodness in the world and not just the worst parts of humanity. *But what if helping Paige ends our friendship, the same way Presley's brother's investigation did?* Martin pushed that thought away. He couldn't leave Paige without protection.

He pushed himself to block out these worries and settle into investigative mode. "Did you register any details about the men who tried to kidnap you?"

"The two that grabbed me were both pretty tall. White." She frowned. "Now that I think about it, they both had dark eyebrows and blue eyes. They weren't twins, but I guess they looked alike in some way."

"Good observation," he said, filing the details away for later consideration. "Does Layla still work for the *Sacramento Chronicle*?"

She nodded. "I guess I should call the police?"

Her voice made her statement into a question, as if she was assessing how that would go.

Martin held back his skepticism. "You can report the attack and see what they say."

He hoped the police could find some way to help, but they had so little information to go on. In his experience, this was the kind of situation where people hired private investigators, mostly because the police couldn't do much unless they knew something about the perpetrators. Paige's were white men dressed in black in a black van, which hardly narrowed down the suspect pool in this area. Getting practical help from the police was a long shot in this situation, but Paige needed to hope for something right now. Also, waiting for them would give him time to get his head around what had just happened and what he was going to do about it. And to get his emotions under control. He felt the warmth of their connection, despite the years since they'd seen each other. There had always been a closeness between them. But he couldn't let that get in the way of helping her.

"We can start with the call," he said.

Paige looked into his eyes. "I can't believe you're really here."

"I'm glad I am," he said, but his thoughts took a more pessimistic turn: If those men were targeting Layla and therefore Paige, they would try again soon. And next time they would be better prepared.

TWO

"I'm sorry for what you went through, Paige," said Officer Mike Brady as he closed his notepad and shoved it into the breast pocket of his uniform. "I'll turn these notes into an official report of the incident back at the station."

"Thanks." Paige blew out a breath, then asked the question that had been on the tip of her tongue since he and Officer Renée Chapman had pulled up in the squad car. "But what can you do for my sister?"

A gust of wind whipped the sprinkle of rain down Main Street as the officers glanced at each other. Mike frowned as he pulled his Ray Bans from where they were perched on his head and gave his blond buzz cut a quick ruffle.

"Her message said she was lying low," he said, pointing to Paige's phone, where she had just played the voicemail for the two officers minutes ago. "She didn't sound in distress so...we need to take her at her word. The incident with a van is likely an unfortunate coincidence."

Paige held back an audible sigh. One advantage to living in a small town was she'd known a good portion of the people since she was small. Renée was a transplant, but Mike was a fellow Clover Valley High School graduate, just a few years ahead of Paige. She knew Mike as a decent guy. But one of the downsides of living in a small town was that… well, everyone knew her, which meant Mike remembered the other three times Paige had come to them with her worries when Layla went missing. The first time, the department had sent out a few cruisers…and found her sister in their cabin, right where she said she'd be. Apparently, she'd just stepped out for a walk when Paige had come to check in. The other two times, they'd advised Paige to wait, and each time Layla had turned up a few days later.

But this time felt different, and Paige had no idea how to convey that the urgency of her uneasiness was more than just sisterly concern. That this was more than just an attack that was a robbery at its core. This was an abduction attempt.

"But that man in the van," she tried. "If he just wanted my purse, why would he try to pull me in? He said he'd been looking for me. Why?"

"It's frightening when something like this happens, and it can be hard to remember. And too often, it doesn't make a lot of sense." Mike patted her on the shoulder. It was supposed to be a friendly gesture, but it felt condescending, especially since he seemed to be ignoring her point.

Martin had been standing quietly to the side, just listening in, but at Mike's last comment, he stepped forward. "I'm treating the threat as real. I saw it."

"Of course," said Renée quickly. "If you see anyone following you, call us immediately."

But what was she supposed to do until then? Paige pushed the wet wisps of hair out of her face, trying to smooth them back into her ponytail. Dusk came early in the mountains, especially when the clouds hung low. The afternoon was growing darker.

"I'm sorry, but we have very little to go on," added Mike. "I'll put out a call for the department to watch for a black van with mud-covered Nevada plates, and we'll alert the Sacramento department about a missing person, but aside from that, there's not a lot we can do except wait."

Paige understood they didn't have much to go on. Still, the police could put a little more effort into looking for Layla. They could do something more…couldn't they? Beside her, Martin was silent.

Mike put on his Ray Bans, the lenses dotted with the drizzling rain, reflecting the thick clouds that hung low over the valley. "If you're worried that this involves your sister, my advice is to also be careful until Layla emerges again. Then she'll tell you what's going on."

Paige bit back the responses that came to mind: Was he suggesting she barricade herself in her house? Or maybe leave town…and not show up for work? At least she had today and tomorrow free before she had to consider that possibility. Either way, she'd be leaving her sister on her own. And Paige's instincts told her Layla was currently in a tight spot—or worse.

Paige was still clutching the envelope in her hands. She had no idea what was on the thumb drive, but considering Mike's response… Well, she wanted to see for herself what was on it first. She noted that Martin hadn't mentioned it, either.

"We'll be on the alert for signs of your purse and the van," said Renee.

"Thanks," she said, trying to control her frustration.

Mike gave her a nod and shook Martin's hand before the two officers turned back to the squad car. Their engine started, and the car slowly made its way back down Main Street, disappearing into the fog.

Paige looked up at Martin. "That was disappointing."

"I had a feeling it might be," he said, his voice gentle. "We all have this idea that we give police whatever evidence we have, and they solve the crime for us. The reality is much less satisfying. Most crimes go unsolved, and it's often because the police need a lot more information to go on than what we have." Martin gave her a wry smile. "Which is why people hire private investigators."

For the first time since he'd appeared today, Martin's expression was a little lighter. She still hadn't gotten used to the seriousness he now carried with him, so different from the lightheartedness she'd loved when they were younger. Maybe it was just the situation? But right now, he looked a bit more like the teenager she had known.

"Are you angling for a job?" she asked, the corners of her mouth tugging up.

He shook his head. "Definitely not. I'm on vacation right now."

Paige swallowed, trying to hide her embarrassment. That was the second rejection he'd given her. She'd meant her comment as a joke, but he'd sounded serious when he'd answered. Of course, Martin wasn't going to solve this for her. She was on her own. She was used to it, but for a moment it had felt so good to lean on someone, even just for a little while. She straightened up, determined to get out of this awkward situation as soon as possible. "Well, then I guess I'll just head back home. But thank you..."

"Wait, Paige."

He rested his hand on her arm, and her heart took off. Slowly, she lifted her gaze and met his dark brown eyes.

"I said I wasn't for hire, but that doesn't mean I won't help you find Layla, if that's what you want." His brow was lined with worry. "I just meant I wouldn't take money to help out a friend."

They were still friends, right? The idea brought the same rush of warmth she'd felt when she'd spotted him across the street, followed by the same embarrassment. Because friends answered their friends' texts. Friends didn't ghost each other, especially after an evening that had felt more like a date than a friend reunion. But right now, she couldn't afford to get hung up on that.

"Well, Mr. PI, what do you suggest?" she asked, trying for some lightness in her voice.

"First of all, I wouldn't suggest going back to your house for more than a few minutes, and definitely not alone," he said. "I'm staying with my parents, and they have a guest bedroom where you can change and get warmed up. Then we can make a plan."

"I want to stop at home for a few things."

Martin looked down at her wet pants and frowned. "We'll need to be quick. They have your purse, so they know where you live. Even if they were after Layla, they're going to be looking for you, too."

Her heart jumped in her chest.

"I didn't think of that," she whispered. Her thoughts were so scattered right now, and it was hard to reason through the details. But she'd have to start focusing.

Martin's expression softened. "You just had a traumatic experience. Give yourself a little grace. I'm here for you."

For now, at least. She closed her eyes and took a long breath. Her sister was missing; she needed to get her fear under control so she could find Layla.

* * *

As Martin followed Paige's Jeep back to her place, the list of reasons why getting involved with her attack wasn't a good idea ran through his head. First, this was supposed to be his vacation, though vacation wasn't quite the right word for what had brought him back home. Rest and recovery was closer, with a heavy emphasis on the recovery part.

There were many things he loved about being a private investigator. He loved that he could help anxious families find answers—and sometimes even peace. As a kid, he'd devoured every mystery he could find, from his father's well-worn Encyclopedia Brown hand-me-downs, the *Detective Mya Dove* books he had picked up for his younger cousins and ended up reading himself, and he'd formed a picture in his mind about the life of a private investigator. Some of it had turned out to be true, like the thrill of weaving clues into answers, the freedom to choose his schedule and the satisfaction of giving people the answers they craved. But there was another part of the job, one that no children's series hinted at, and it had worn on him since he'd graduated from San Francisco State. As a private investigator, Martin sometimes saw the worst of humanity.

He had formed his own sort of policy, his own code of ethics that went far beyond meeting the client's needs. He would help if he saw others in need—he had to find a way to help them, too. This was the only way he had been able to do this job. He couldn't ignore the other things going on, just because they weren't paying clients. And so he had done that. He had contacted everyone from social services to homeless shelters to rehab clinics. And this had allowed him to rest at night. It allowed him to feel like he was leaving the place better than he had found it, even the times when the news he was taking back to the clients was the absolute worst.

But then Presley had come to him, begging for Martin to help his family find his brother Amos, and Martin couldn't help but get involved. He'd worked through two nights, and when he'd found Amos in the Tenderloin district in the midst of a mental health breakdown, he'd called the family immediately. To Martin's shock, the family turned on him. His mother denied that her son had any mental health struggles and would never go to the Tenderloin, notorious for drug use. Then, when Martin sent photos, she told Martin to tell Amos he needed to shape up before he came home. Presley's reaction wasn't much better. Martin had looked at Amos, so clearly suffering, and called the homeless outreach team, and the family never forgave Martin for interfering.

"We asked you to find him. Not embarrass the family," Presley had said.

But how could Martin not help someone in need? After that, the grief and pain wore on him. Everything felt personal. Sometimes his cases pointed to relatives so mired in hopelessness, to partners cheating on each other and to families hiding secrets that were worse than cheating. While in the beginning, he had tried to simply turn off the feelings, Martin had come to the conclusion that he wasn't the kind of person who could do that. Day after day, week after week, year after year, the cases that revealed people's most heartbreaking moments took a toll.

Apparently, that toll had seeped into his voice, which was why a phone call with his father last month had ended with the words, "Son, you need to come home for a while, and I won't take no for an answer."

Martin so rarely refused his parents' requests, and he could hear in his father's tone that this wasn't the time to start. Eddie Hosey didn't mess around. When his mother had made the US National Ski Team, his father found a way for both of them to move to the Tahoe area, combining his business skills with Martin's mother's local celebrity clout to create an adventure sports shop that lasted long after his mother had won the Olympic Bronze medal and retired. When his father wanted him to help lead trips for Hosey's Outdoor Adventure Sports, Martin didn't think twice about doing it. And two days ago, when Martin had walked into his childhood home, and his father had taken one look at him, handed him the Arts section of the *New York Times* and said, "The only mysteries you should be solving this week are in the crossword," Martin had no intention of doing otherwise…until now.

His PI senses were on alert as he parked his black Toyota RAV4 in front of the garage where Paige had parked her Jeep. He followed her out of the garage and along the path to the front door of the apartment building. It wasn't big, two stories with six garages, surrounded by a handful of identical buildings. The exterior was brick on the bottom, then clad in wood panels, painted a medium brown and angled in a way that reminded him of the 1970s. Everything about this place reminded him of the 1970s, though it had been kept up pretty well.

Mostly. Martin frowned up at the burnt-out porch light at her unit. *None of your business*, he told himself. Paige was an adult, perfectly capable of dealing with her living situation. Even if the isolation of her place was giving him a bad feeling. He hadn't seen anyone around when they'd pulled up, but night was falling.

Martin was glad to see that Maggie stuck close by as they walked into the building and up the dimly lit staircase to the second floor. He comforted himself with the fact that the dog would have certainly told them if someone was around the corner. Still, he could feel uneasiness radiate from Paige, as if she was struggling with similar fears.

"Good thing I keep my keys in my pockets," she said as they faced the wooden door marked 203. "I got tired of losing them in my purse."

A flash of a younger version of her popped into his head: Paige taking everything out of her ski bag because she couldn't find one of her gloves...again. He felt the corners of his mouth twitch in amusement. "So the lesson you're taking away from this is that disorganization pays off?"

"Absolutely."

She stuck her key into the lock, but before she turned it, Martin rested his hand on her arm. "Let Maggie go in first. And don't turn on the lights."

The hint of humor in her expression faded, and she nodded. She opened the door, and the dog bounded in, heading straight for the kitchen. Martin peered around the corner and spotted the dog with her head ducked into the water bowl. She lapped the water noisily, then turned as if to say, *What are you waiting for?*

"Should we go in?" asked Paige.

Martin nodded. "I'll keep an eye on the window while you gather what you need."

Paige disappeared down the apartment's dark hallway, and Martin headed for the living room window that overlooked the parking lot, positioning himself in a dark armchair. Maggie followed him, and he scratched her head as he peered out. It was quiet outside. The fog and drizzle formed a hazy mist that cloaked the forest across the street, so that the treetops looked almost like they were floating. Headlights flashed through the mist, and Martin strained to see the car that approached. It was a black van. He froze, keeping himself behind the curtain.

"I think they might be here," Martin called down the dark hallway, keeping his voice low.

Paige came running from the bedroom with a duffel bag in her hand.

"Stay out of sight," he added.

She nodded and squatted next to the dog, hugging her. "I almost flipped the light switch out of habit," she whispered. "Thank God I didn't."

"Let's see what they do."

The vehicle pulled into the building's lot and slowed to a stop, not far from Martin's SUV. He strained for a view of the driver, but the window was shrouded in mist. The van idled there with a dull hum that didn't come close to drowning out the hitch in Paige's breath. He waited. Waited. Finally, they pulled out and slowly drove away.

Martin let out an audible breath. "We need to get out of here. Let's take my car."

The car was silent as they drove through the winding roads of Clover Valley. Paige lived up in the mountains a bit, but Martin's parents lived closer to Main Street, just over the river, in a big old house that felt one step away from a log cabin. As they pulled into his parents' driveway Martin could see his father through the front windows, making dinner in the kitchen. He had no idea how his parents were going to take the news that he had, in fact, stumbled into a case—exactly what he'd said he wouldn't do.

He caught up with Paige and took the duffel bag she'd

packed while Paige clipped on Maggie's leash. "You sure your parents will be okay with another dog?"

"Yes, especially since Junior will love Maggie." Junior, his family's chocolate Lab, had been Martin's rescue project in the beginning, but by the time he moved to San Francisco, the dog was so bonded to his parents and their enormous property that Martin didn't have the heart to take Junior away. Especially considering the irregular hours his job demanded. "It will be fine until we figure out what to do."

"At least I got to spray off her paws back at my place."

Paige kept Maggie on a short leash as they walked to the front door. Junior stood in his place by the front window, tail wagging.

"Time to put your best paw forward, Maggie," whispered Paige as Martin pulled open the front door.

Her dog gave a short yip of greeting, and Junior crouched on the front hallway floor, tail up in play position. Martin stroked his dog as Maggie approached, sniffing. Junior stood up and sniffed back.

"Martin, is that you?"

His mother's voice floated down the hallway. He took one more look at the dogs, then back down the hallway.

"Do you have this under control?" he asked.

Paige nodded. "I think so."

"I'll be right back," he said and headed to the kitchen.

The house was built in typical Tahoe style, with high ceilings and wood beams, a big fireplace and pine shelves that spilled over with his mother's favorite romances and mysteries. There were family photos everywhere, some packed with aunts, uncles and cousins and others, just the three of them. His favorite was the one of him and his father in the matching pajamas his mother had given then for Christmas when he was sixteen. They were laughing at each other, and Martin looked like an almost-identical version of his father, just a little skinnier. It had been a fun Christmas that year. Each photo, book, each blanket draped over the back of a chair made the place feel like a home, unlike Martin's sparse, drafty flat in one of San Francisco's pre-earthquake buildings near the Panhandle.

His father stood over the cutting board, chopping garlic, and his mother was examining a box of pasta from the cupboard.

"Is that another dog I heard?" said his father with a hint of amusement in his voice. "Don't tell me you picked up a stray again."

"Don't get your hopes up, Eddie," said his mother with a wry smile. "You know you love Junior like he's your second child."

His father chuckled. "I don't know what you're talking about."

His parents had been married for thirty-one years, and the warmth and comfortable banter that still thrived between the two of them was a balm every time he visited home. How did they stay upbeat when the world gave everyone so many reasons not to? It was a reminder that good things, important things survived, even amidst all the sadness he'd witnessed.

"The dog belongs to Paige Addison," he said. "She's here, too."

His mother raised her eyebrows, and the corners of his father's mouth twitched up.

"That's a name I haven't heard in a while," Eddie said.

Mercifully, they kept the rest of their thoughts to themselves, but he could see from the looks on both their faces that when the three of them were alone again, he'd get a few prying questions. He'd been mostly out of touch with the Fabulous Five for years, aside from their annual reunions, and every time his parents asked about them, he brushed off their questions. How could he explain that hearing about Paige's troubles was exactly what he'd dreaded, exactly why he'd stayed away? His job was already heartbreaking. The only solution was to find ways to harden himself against the relentless battering of seeing people at their most desperate. But when it was Paige who was desperate, when the connection was personal? Martin was afraid his heart would break in ways that couldn't be repaired. When she and Layla had moved away, it had felt as if the whole world got a little dimmer. He'd missed them both so much, though it felt different with Paige. Even harder. And still, he had brought her to his parents' home. Still, he wanted to protect her. He had no idea what to do with these two warring feelings inside him, let alone how to explain them to his parents.

"Layla's in some sort of trouble, and it's spilling over to Paige," he said in a low voice. "Can she stay in the guest bedroom for the night while we figure out what to do next?"

The teasing look faded from his father's face as he took in the seriousness of Martin's tone. Or maybe he'd already made the connection to what this meant for Martin's "vacation."

"Of course. She's always welcome here."

Nails scraped on the well-worn wooden floor as the dogs raced in, with Paige following behind Maggie, still holding onto her leash. Martin's mother set aside the pasta box she was holding and crossed the kitchen. She wrapped her arms around Paige for a quick squeeze, then dropped to her knees in front of Maggie. "Who's this?"

Paige grinned. "Maggie, who is probably going to embarrass me with her manners."

"As long as you don't give Junior any ideas," said his mother, pointing her comment to Maggie as she scratched the dog behind her ears. "He's already in enough trouble as it is."

As his father hugged Paige, he could see the worry lines on his friend's face disappear. His parents peppered her with questions about her job as they cooked dinner. Martin set the table, just listening, while Paige played with the dogs and compared the snow at different resorts this season with them. The scene felt so natural, so much like back in high school, and yet a part of him didn't feel fully present. He had felt this way more often these days, detached, and he wasn't sure what to do with it.

As they sat down at the table and joined hands for grace, Martin glanced across the table at Paige. Her eyes were closed, her chin lowered as his father spoke the blessing in his deep rich voice.

"Amen," she whispered when he finished, keeping her eyes closed for an extra moment. Was she praying for her sister as well? Prayer had slowly disappeared from his life, much in the way that regular sleep, optimism and vacation had. His church attendance was sparse, too, having been an obligation more than a deliberate choice before the monthly Sunday family gatherings at his grandparents' towering Victorian in Oakland. Yet right now, as he studied Paige, he felt a lift in his chest. A connection to his older self. But the moment was gone as soon as it came, and that feeling of distance returned.

"It's so nice to catch up with you," said his mother as she twirled strands of spaghetti around her fork. "But Martin says your sister is in some kind of trouble."

Of course, he should have known his mother would get to the heart of the matter. She was nothing if not direct.

His father studied Paige with concern. "Is there anything we can help with?"

"Thanks so much for your concern, but I know almost nothing about what's going on. I haven't spoken to Layla in two weeks, and her phone has been offline for three days. I can't find her, but her truck is still parked at our cabin."

"Someone tried to grab Paige off Main Street this afternoon, right across from the store," added Martin. "I was too late to help."

His mother's eyes widened, and his father froze in his chair. If they hadn't understood the reason behind Paige's visit before, they did now. *I'm sorry*, he added silently to them.

"Martin was there for me." Paige glanced at him, her eyes filled with gratitude.

He felt another tiny lift inside him that his being with her had eased her fears. This was why he'd offered to help, he told himself, even though another reason he shouldn't get involved was clambering for his attention. It was hard enough to watch strangers struggling through awful surprises and difficult revelations, but this was Paige. It was impossible to ignore the overwhelming call from deep inside to keep the people close to him safe. Which meant that, despite all the risks, despite knowing the truth had the power to upend people's lives, he was going to help her find Layla. And then he could back out of her life again until he'd fixed this broken part inside him. He searched for a way to convey all these thoughts to his parents.

"I need to go back to the cabin and find where Layla went," said Paige.

Martin almost choked on his forkful of pasta. "What?"

His stomach sank as he took in her expression. It was no longer filled with fear and confusion, the way it had been when the van sped away. Instead, she looked determined. If Paige was anything close to her high school self, she wasn't going to change her mind.

"Something's going on, and you heard the police. There's not a lot they'll do at this point." Paige lowered her eyes to her plate, but he was almost sure he saw tears forming. "But my sister is in trouble. I can feel it."

"Going back to the cabin doesn't sound like a good idea." Martin was trying to keep his voice calm, despite the heavy thump of his heart.

"I need to get there before the rain that's supposed to come in tomorrow, in case there are footprints or…some sort of clues." She frowned. "These men shouldn't know about the cabin. It's still under my grandmother's last name, not ours, and her address is in New Mexico. That's why Layla uses the place as a retreat."

Martin raised a skeptical eyebrow. "They shouldn't know about it unless they have done a lot of digging. Or have some sort of local connection."

"You don't have to get yourself any more involved in this, Martin," she said softly. "You've already done more than enough by inviting me here, with your family. I'm grateful."

Martin looked up at his father, expecting reproach, but instead he found what looked more like sympathy. Maybe his father understood him better than Martin thought. After all, this was a man who had shaped his life around supporting his wife when she needed it. His mother was the first Black woman to win an Olympic gold in the giant slalom, and his father had left a good job and moved away from his friends and family in Oakland to support Martin's mother's career in the mountains. Not that Paige was anything like a wife to him, but they had once been close, and at their dinner in Sacramento, that closeness had come back. It was what had driven him away, but it was also what pulled him in. Maybe he didn't need to speak the words for his father to know what was going through his mind: he couldn't leave Paige to pursue her sister on her own.

"I'll come with you," he said.

Paige nodded. "Thank you. I just want to search the place better than I did the last time."

"The storm is coming in tomorrow. I heard they're expecting road closures. There are a lot of burn scars around here after the last two fire seasons," his father added.

The table fell silent, and his parents exchanged glances. His mother finally broke the silence.

"Sounds like you two have a lot to discuss," said his mother in that voice she'd used countless times to smooth over the squabbles that inevitably came with growing up with three outspoken siblings. "But first, who wants some apple pie?"

After dessert, Paige offered to take care of the dishes. Martin's parents headed upstairs instead of settling into their usual evening spot on the sofa in front of the fireplace, leaving him alone to talk with his friend.

"I can't imagine your parents are thrilled about you coming with me," said Paige as she slid a plate into the bottom rack of the dishwasher.

"They're not thrilled about my career choice in general," he said as he scooped the remainder of the pasta into a glass storage dish. "My father wants me to take it easy. He made me promise to leave behind anything related to private investigation—no computer and definitely no gun. He's got a thing about guns."

She stopped and turned to look at him. "You really shouldn't come with me."

"He also knows that I can't stop myself from helping a friend."

Paige frowned, and Martin sensed she was going to argue, so he added, "I'm in, and I'm not changing my mind."

Paige shooed Maggie away from the dishwasher and tucked a lock of hair behind her ear. "We can quickly check the area for clues and then leave. I came and went last time with no problem."

Martin held back the pessimism that was on the tip of his tongue. They'd find out how easy it would be soon enough.

"I hope it goes smoothly. But I think we should leave Maggie with my parents, just in case," he said, sliding into the stool at the kitchen island's counter.

She was quiet for a moment, then said, "I want to see what's on the thumb drive."

"No laptop, remember?" Martin frowned. "But I think my parents' desktop might still work."

A few minutes later, they gathered in front of it, and Martin brushed a layer of dust off the keyboard and pressed the power button. Five minutes later, they were still waiting for it to load.

He flashed her a wry smile. "Updates."

After another five minutes, the first of 127 pages was loading on the screen. It looked like notes from an interview, with lots of abbreviations. There was a list of property lot numbers with companies listed afterwards, all with vague names like Sierra Holdings, and there were more lists of banks and PO box addresses.

Paige squinted at the screen. "She seems to be making connections between different properties and companies, and she seems to be tracking PO box addresses. I'd suggest we look each of these things up, but I'm afraid we'll be up all night."

Martin sighed. She was right. "After we go to your cabin tomorrow, I'll go back to your apartment for your laptop, okay?"

She nodded. "Thanks. Should we leave the thumb drive here. Or do you think it might put your parents in danger?"

Martin considered her question. "I don't think so. Whoever tried to kidnap you doesn't know your connection to me, so they don't know to check here." He searched her face, noting how her dark brown eyes were clouded with worry. "Now, tell me everything you remember from today."

But before she could start, her phone rang. She answered, and Martin could hear bits and pieces of the voice at the other end. "Mike...police..."

He got up, instinctively moving closer, and Paige lowered the phone and turned on the speaker so he could listen, too. When she met his gaze, the fear had returned to her eyes. "Have you found my sister?"

"I'm sorry. We haven't," came Mike's voice. "But we found your purse. It was in a snow pile on the side of the road. The money and bank cards are still in your wallet, but your driver's license is missing."

Martin frowned. The van they saw in front of her apartment had been most likely there for her, then.

Paige closed her eyes. "Thank you," she said after a pause. "I—I'll be there to pick it up tomorrow."

She ended the call and met Martin's gaze. "They were trying to pull me into that van. And then they found my apartment. Whatever they want, they're still after it."

Martin swiped a hand over his face and shook his head. If Paige's guess was correct, that the men had initially been looking for Layla, they now needed to assume that the men would be looking for Paige, too. It wouldn't take much to connect their identical appearances and suspect that Paige might have information about where Layla was and what she was doing. "Even if they're after Layla, those men will see you as just as much of a threat as she is."

THREE

Paige squinted through the windshield as Michael steered his RAV4 around the familiar curves of the mountain road the next morning. A heavy wet fog had woven its way up the mountainside, leaving a constant mist on the windshield and cloaking the surrounding forest in gray clouds. She usually loved this weather, but today it took on a more sinister tone. Was her sister somewhere out there, alone? Was someone chasing her?

They'd passed a few trucks parked in the dirt turnoffs on the side of the road, and they had met one lone driver on the assent, a single man in a blue pickup who didn't look twice in their direction. Paige watched to make sure, and even after that truck passed, her whole body was tense, on alert. What was she even looking for? Someone who still hadn't changed from yesterday's head-to-toe kidnapper uniform? The truth was she didn't know what she should be looking for, and that made the dim morning all the more eerie.

Everything she'd told Martin about the situation was true—the visit to the cabin, the attack on Main Street and her complete bewilderment about who was behind it. But last night, as she'd gone over her day with him, she'd left out one important detail: the door to the cabin had been ajar when she'd arrived. It hadn't been a conscious choice, just a slip of her memory that had come back as she lay in bed, her mind going over the events of the day on endless repeat. But when she'd remembered this morning, she hesitated to bring it up. What if he decided it was too dangerous and pressured her not to go? The door could be a red herring. Maybe Layla hadn't shut the door tightly enough, and a sharp gust of wind blew it open? Her gut told her that wasn't likely, but how likely were any of the events of the last twenty-four hours?

"How close are we?" asked Martin. "The weather isn't going to hold up for much longer."

He gestured into the forest, through the heavy fog, where the sky was growing darker by the minute.

"We're not far," she said with a quick glance in his direction. Martin was dressed in black rain gear with an orange cap, a nod to the year-round wild boar hunting allowed in the park forests in the area. His father had insisted. Hunters were required to stick to the designated national forest boundaries, but wild boars didn't care about boundaries and, unfortunately, hunters in pursuit of their trails didn't always, either. Especially in her family's part of the mountain, where a few of the properties to the north had been all but abandoned since the Gold Rush mines closed, and others had been knocked out in the fire last summer.

"We're coming to the bend where cell phone reception ends," she said, pointing into the mist. "It's the last place Layla's phone—"

Her words died as she spotted a silver truck, a big one with a cab that seated five, pulled off on the side of the road, just before the bend.

"Do you recognize that car?" Martin's voice was full of urgency.

She shook her head. "It's close to the cabin. Within walking distance. And this property is private."

Martin didn't look happy about that piece of information. "We should park out of sight, not in your driveway. Just in case."

"Good idea."

After a few more twists and hairpin turns, she pointed out the driveway. Martin slowed as they passed, and she squinted into the fog. Nothing looked out of the ordinary from this distance, just the same muddy tracks her own jeep had left, though she couldn't be sure. Martin continued around the next bend, then slowed to a stop on a muddy turnoff. They were both silent as she tucked her hair into her own orange hat. It made their approach less subtle, but his father had insisted.

"Your dad was really worried about us getting shot," she said gently.

"Me, in particular. You look like a typical cabin owner up here." He gave her a sideways glance. "I don't. The hat suggests I'm here to hunt. Not sneak around on someone else's property. Not a threat."

Oh. The weight of his words settled into her. She had been so focused on finding her sister that she hadn't registered that wandering around on people's property was more dangerous for him than for her. "I'm sorry. I didn't consider the extra risk you're taking on. I should have thought about that."

Martin gave her a soft smile. "You don't have to be sorry for the way the world works. I was aware of the circumstances when I chose to come with you."

All the circumstances except for the front door of the cabin. Paige bit her lip. Should she tell him now? Before she could find the words, Martin opened his door and climbed out. She rushed to follow. The rain dusted her dark gray all-weather jacket as they crossed the two-lane mountain road and entered the forest. Tall pines rose up from the steep slope. The ground was dotted with a scattering of scraggly bushes clinging to clumps of dirt. Long thin needles lined the path as they descended into fog, still and dark, like the calm before the storm.

"You lead the way," said Martin in a low voice. "And tell me if anything looks suspicious. Even if it might be nothing. Even if you're not sure."

Paige's conscience nagged at her.

"There is one thing," she said hesitantly.

He stopped and looked at her expectantly, eyebrows raised.

"There was something a little…off about the cabin when I visited. Someone left the door open, and I can't imagine my sister making that mistake."

"You just remembered that?" he asked skeptically.

"Not exactly." Her cheeks heated. "I remembered it after I hung up the phone with the police last night and we went to bed."

"And you didn't tell me this morning because you would make me more skeptical about this plan."

She cringed. "Something like that."

He studied her for a moment but said nothing. Was he assessing how much he should trust her? As a friend, she held him in the highest regard, and the idea that he might find her less than trustworthy made her gut twist. Her face heated with embarrassment.

"I'm sorry," she added.

His expression softened, and he gave her a nod of acknowledgment.

They trudged through the wet forest floor as raindrops

pattered on the trees and landed on her jacket. The mountainside was steep, with jutting boulders that made it difficult to see around the curve of the mountain, even on a clear day. Most of the forest floor was brown and soft, but there were hints of spring green poking up through the dirt. Her feet sunk into the soft earth as they followed an animal trail parallel to the road. She dodged icy clumps of snow, lying in watery heaps.

The rumble of a car engine echoed over the mountainside, and she looked up at Martin. He glanced in the direction of the road but said nothing. The car was coming closer. They weren't far from the road, but the fog was dense. If the driver looked down the mountainside, could they make out the orange caps? The only close cover was the thin trunk of a tree, narrower than she was, so Paige moved behind it and watched as the headlights flashed in their direction. Her heart thumped in her chest as the car slowed. Rounded the curve. Continued. She glanced over at Martin, just as clumsily hidden as she was, as the rumble of the engine faded.

"I think we're okay," he said in a low voice.

Paige blew out a sigh of relief, but her heart still hammered in her chest.

They rounded a familiar stack of thick granite boulders and came to her driveway. She pointed to the tracks that her Jeep had made the day before.

"I parked here, and these are my footprints," she said in a low voice. "I don't see anyone else's."

"Good to know. Though this isn't the only way to get to the cabin." He gestured at the open forest that surrounded them.

"I suppose entering through the front door wouldn't be the most subtle tactic."

"Neither are these hats." The corners of Martin's mouth kicked up into a wry smile.

"If anyone is here, they'll see us right away."

He nodded. "Probably, but we should still stay hidden as long as possible. Plus, you'd be surprised the kinds of mistakes people make when they're trying to sneak around."

He started forward, following the driveway, keeping his voice low. "Sometimes people's carelessness gives me comfort. Despite the amount of dishonesty some people are capable of, they aren't good at it. And it makes me think that it's just not in most people's nature to be good at deception. That's much better than believing that people aren't good."

There was so much behind that statement that she recognized. How many times had she struggled between hope and despair, with wanting to believe the best in people, even when she felt foolish and naive for it? Paige wanted to ask him more, but now wasn't the time for a discussion. Later, she thought, though when was later? She'd more than gotten the hint that he was trying to distance himself from her. He'd also made it sound like it wasn't personal, but that somehow made it worse.

She followed Martin down the driveway and around the boulders that separated her family's cabin from the road. The rain was picking up, landing in fat drops on her coat and on the muddy driveway in front of her. As they rounded the last one, Martin froze. "Someone's here."

"The red truck is my sister's," she said.

He nodded, but there was still a cloud of wariness in his expression. "It just...feels like someone's here."

A wave of unguarded excitement filled her. "Maybe it's Layla. Maybe she came back."

In her mind, the scenario took form. Maybe someone had approached the cabin and Layla had left for a while but returned? There were holes in that theory, starting with the fact that if their cabin had indeed been discovered by someone, Layla likely wouldn't want to return. But Paige needed to choose hope. What else did she have? *Please, Lord, let her be okay.* Her heart thumped faster in her chest as the cabin appeared through the mist.

"Let's circle the property before going in," said Martin. "Remember to keep your eyes open for anything that sticks out."

"Good idea," she said, despite the disappointment that flooded through her at Martin's more levelheaded plan. Her limbs were tingling with the urge to run inside, to check for her sister.

They stepped off the driveway, away from the clearing, where their cabin stood, and into the forest. The scent of wet earth and pine needles was everywhere, and the trees rustled in the wind. The cabin was built on a relatively flat stretch on the descending hump of one of the peaks. Just beyond the crop of granite, the mountain continued its steep decline. They traveled a bit down the slope, so the living room windows were barely in sight.

"Walk in my footsteps if you can," said Martin in a low voice, so she did, watching as he avoided bushes and stepped over twigs and branches, finding the soft ground. They made their way along the property, keeping the cabin in sight. She tried to get a better look into the cabin windows, but the foggy haze darkened the glass. There was no sign of movement or lights. Everything was shrouded in mist. The rain pattered on the ground around them, covering the swishing sound of her all-weather coat as she walked. At least she hoped so.

Paige was so busy looking at the house and at the path

in front of her that she almost bumped into Martin when he came to a stop in front of her.

"What is it?" she whispered.

Martin turned to her. "Footprints."

She came up next to him and followed his gaze. In front of them was a path of prints. Some seemed to point downhill and toward the north, toward the edge of their property, where the forest came to an abrupt end and the burn scar began. Others headed back toward the house.

Paige stepped into the path and set her own size six hiking boot in one of the prints. It fit exactly.

"Not many men have feet this small. Definitely not the guys who had jumped out of the van, considering how tall they were," she said. "But Layla wears my size. These could be hers, and some of them lead back to the cabin."

Her heart thumped harder. Did that mean her sister was close?

"I have to go in there, Martin," she said.

He frowned at her.

"Something's wrong," she insisted. "I can feel it. I need to go in."

She had tried not to let him see this, tried not to let on the depth of her fear, but she couldn't hold it back.

"Let me go first," Martin finally said.

She looked into his dark eyes. They were guarded, so unlike the teenager she had known.

She shook her head. "I don't want you to take that risk."

"Everything around here is risky." He gave her a serious look. "I'll check it out, make sure no one is in there, while you keep watch. The moment you see something, anything, yell to me. I'll leave the back door open so I can hear you."

She swallowed. He was going to take yet another risk for

her, probably against his better judgment. Still, she handed him the key. "Thank you."

"Always."

He held her gaze, and for a moment, she saw a flash of the Martin she had known, that mix of confidence, determination and empathy. She felt a bit of her discomfort over dragging him into her troubles fade. But the look on his face was gone just as quickly as it had appeared.

He scanned the property. The rain was falling harder, and the boulders and rocky outcrops that encircled the cabin were a dark blur. After a last glance at her, he started up the slope and across the open space. She watched his tall broad figure fade into the rain. The orange cap glowed through the mist, making her even more nervous. She squinted across the yard, looking for movement, but the rain and the wind made it hard to see anything clearly.

He reached the back porch, and at the top of the steps, Martin looked over his shoulder, scanning the area. Then he turned to the door, fiddled with the lock and disappeared inside. The wind was picking up, blowing branches and splattering rain against her face. She wiped off a drip from the tip of her nose and studied the surroundings, starting from her left, through the forest and across the open space. As she turned to look over her right shoulder, a flash of black material moved just beyond a dense pine tree only a few yards away. She whipped around and opened her mouth to scream, but before she could get the sound out, a hand clamped over her mouth. Panic rose to a fever pitch, paralyzing her. She had been horribly right. Layla's pursuers had found their cabin. And now they'd found her.

"Which twin is this?"

"I think it's the one from town," muttered the voice behind her. "You go after the man."

Paige watched in horror as a man in a black jacket and black face mask stepped out from behind the pine tree and ran up the incline, straight toward the cabin. Toward Martin. *No.*

She squirmed and kicked. The man grasped her around her waist with his other hand, cutting off movement of her left arm. But her right arm was free. Both the bulk of their clothes and her slippery jacket could work in her favor if she could get her footing.

"That's enough. The boss just wants to look at the information you have and come to a mutually beneficial understanding with your sister and anyone else involved. This can all be civilized. Just tell us where your sister is."

Paige's body came alive with a new flutter of hope. Her sister was still free. That thought gave her a burst of energy, and she kicked harder, fighting him off. He grunted as her elbow found his side. She ducked her chin and twisted her neck until his hand slipped from her mouth.

"Martin!" she screamed. "Someone's coming."

But her voice was swallowed by the wind.

Martin worked alone, and as he walked across the bright green grassy clearing and climbed the steps to the back entrance to the cabin, he was remembering all the reasons why. Because he could manage watching his own back and assessing his own risks, the ones he was willing to take. But his usual risk assessment had been thrown off-kilter the moment he'd stepped out of the car. How did he assess acceptable risk when Paige was next to him? Suddenly, every movement he caught out of the corner of his eye was a threat, and the high-alert signals coursing through him wouldn't stop. His equilibrium was off, and he had no idea how to right it again.

Which put both his friend and him even more at risk.

When he reached the top of the stairs, something made him whip around and squint through the rain. Had Paige just called for him? He spotted her orange hat exactly where he'd left her. False alarm. The rain pelted at his back as he turned to the cabin door, slipped the key in the lock and stepped inside. The hallway was dark and eerily still. Though Paige seemed to think that Layla might be inside, Martin was praying he wouldn't find her here. If she hadn't appeared by now, that couldn't mean anything good. It was one of the primary reasons he'd left Paige alone in the forest, against his better judgment. The situation was giving him all sorts of bad vibes, and right now he wasn't sure he could trust his own senses.

He peered through the tiny back hallway and into the kitchen—

"Martin! Someone's coming."

He froze. Was that her, or were the wind and his fears whispering in his ear again? Before he could make a conscious decision, he turned and headed back toward the exit. As he rounded the corner, rain smacking at his face, he saw—too late—a man running up the porch stairs with a gun in his hand. Martin lifted his hands as they collided, and the gun went off. He held onto the man, and they tumbled down the hard wooden steps together. Martin landed on his side in the wet grass, still holding the man. He felt nothing but adrenaline as he struggled to turn the man on his stomach and stay on top of him.

Martin wasn't always the biggest man, but he was usually the fastest, and he'd had enough training to know how to use that to his advantage. He'd caught this guy off guard, but it wouldn't be long before the surprise wore off. He rolled the guy face down in the grass and twisted the man's left arm behind his back. As he tightened his grip, he grabbed the gun with his right hand, pointing it down toward the ground, pulling it loose.

No guns, son. His father's words from late last night rattled through his head. *I understand why you're getting involved in this, but you know how I feel about guns.*

Martin pushed that thought to the back of his mind and shoved the gun into the back of the waistband of his pants. Then he pulled the man's other arm behind his back and stretched the arms of the guy's thin rain jacket enough to get some slack.

"I'm down," called the man. He struggled less now that Martin had his gun, so he pulled hard on both jacket arms until they slipped down his arms. Then he tied the loose material in a knot behind they guy's back. The man was disarmed and subdued, at least for a bit. Good enough for now.

He climbed off the guy and headed straight for Paige. Another man in a black coat and a ski mask was wrestling her into submission, despite her kicks and struggles. Martin felt a surge of protective energy rush through him as he raced through the pelting rain, praying that she wasn't harmed. Just before he reached them, one of her kicks connected, and the man reared back. Martin took advantage of the momentum and threw his arms around the man, pushing him to the side. The guy tumbled off Paige and onto the ground, and Martin fell on top of him, landing hard.

"Run!" he yelled.

She scrambled to her feet. But instead of running in the direction of his car, parked on the side of the road, she took off on the muddy footpath, into the darkness of the mountain.

FOUR

Paige sprinted along the muddy path. Her heart pounded, and her legs felt strangely detached. She couldn't feel any of her body. All she could feel was fear. The gun had gone off, and Martin had been shot. He'd been so close to the other man that she was almost sure of it. And yet still, he was there, behind her, keeping up with her as she sprinted down the trail.

Her feet slipped in the mud as she scrambled farther away. The fog was heavy, and the sky was a dark gray cloud as it hit the mountainside, releasing its pent-up rain. In front of her, there was only mist and trees. Behind her, she heard the squish of Martin's feet hitting the mucky ground. They had to get away, somehow disappear on the mountain, into the fog.

It took everything she had not to turn and search for the wound that he must have. How was he running? If he was bleeding, he couldn't make it for long. She wouldn't have made it far in her career as a home health care worker if she had been squeamish about wounds, but this was different. If she saw his injury, she knew she would give up. She had pulled her friend into this disaster, the man she had trusted with her life so many times back in high school, the man with equal depths of humor and compassion. The idea that he'd been shot was enough to make all the energy in her body run dry. *Please, Lord, help him.* She knew she would crumble to the ground if she saw the evidence that something had happened to him. If she gave up, what would happen to her sister?

She focused on that. She focused on the fact that Layla's car was parked in the driveway. The only way out was on foot, so her sister must be near. And the one good thing about those men showing up was that she was now almost sure they hadn't caught Layla yet…though there had been three total from the van, two that grabbed her and a driver. Where was the other guy? Were there more? What if their associates had caught Layla but couldn't tell the men Paige and Martin had just encountered because they were out of cell phone range?

She reminded herself to keep her faith. Because this was part of faith, not getting pulled into the fear, the sadness that could overwhelm a person in times like this. That trust in God was a trust that there was a way out. Paige's panic receded a little with that thought.

"Now's the time to take off our hats." Martin's voice came from behind her, low but surprisingly steady, bringing her back to the present reality.

"Good point. Give me a minute." She slowed to a walk and whipped off her orange hunting hat, trying to shove it into the pocket of her jacket. Her hands shook as she fumbled with the zipper.

"How bad is it?" she asked.

"They won't be stalled for long," said Martin, his breath so close behind her. His voice had sounded strong, without that tight bite that came with pain, the one she'd heard from patients too many times. He didn't sound on the brink of collapse.

"How bad is your...injury?" She couldn't quite bring herself to say wound, let alone gunshot. Still, the guilt coursed through her. She had brought him into this, and right now, they were so far from help.

He gave a little grunt of a laugh. "Definitely could've been worse."

The lightness of his answer opened up another possibility, and with it, a burst of energy pushed her forward through the trail. It felt like hope. "You...weren't shot?"

"No." There was alarm in his voice, like he now understood what was going on in her mind. "Thank God, no."

"Thank God," she echoed, her prayer ringing with relief. He wasn't bleeding. This thought drove her forward as she stepped out of the green forest and into the burn scar from last summer's fire.

The fire had raced up the mountains, spreading in one direction, then another. The whole forest was at the mercy of the changing winds, and the fires and the dry heat created a cauldron of new weather patterns that washed across the mountain. There was no reason why some things were saved, and some things were not. A slight change in wind, and her cabin would've disappeared. And yet it hadn't. Last summer's fire had shot up the mountain, leaving a strip of burnt remains as the wind blew west, until it came to an end at the rocky peaks. On the far side, a wide clearing for utility lines had acted as an unintentional fire line. That had saved the forests farther north. But it had turned this area into a wasteland.

Once this slope of the mountain had been covered in a thick patch of tall trees, but now there were just a few jagged monuments to the forest, the charred remains, splintered and fallen, dark in the rain and mountain fog. The water coming down made rivers and deep gullies across the path. Yet another threat.

Paige stepped over a burnt log, and dodged another one, trying to ignore the uprooted trees that surrounded them. This was dangerous territory. The snow was melting, sinking between all the broken roots of the devastated trees. If those roots didn't hold the soil together, the ground became more and more unstable.

"Where are we going?" he asked.

She pushed her fears out of the way and focused on the fact that Martin was okay. His breaths were steady behind her, and she felt a surge of warmth for her friend. But his question jolted her back into the present. She had no plan, and her scattered mind was in no state to make one by herself. They needed to go somewhere safe, somewhere out of the rain so they could discuss what to do.

The landscape of the mountain spread out in her mind, carefully etched from fall hikes with her grandmother and summers of exploration with her sister. The properties on both sides of theirs were large and mostly uninhabited. To the south, it was mostly forest, with a cabin that hadn't been inhabited since before Paige was born. The roof had collapsed long ago, and the floorboards weren't in better condition. It might have been a good place to seek shelter if it weren't in the opposite direction from where they were currently headed. Also, it was uphill, and the pitch of the mountain in this area would make for a very slow ascent.

A fire had torn through the property to the north the previous summer, taking with it the cabin and the strip of forest where they were currently running. The only place on that property that was out of the rain was an abandoned mine shaft down the slope, left from the early 1900s. There was a road about a half mile downhill that led to a newer subdivision of upscale homes a few miles farther, where Justine, their childhood friend had a home, and in the other direction was a long road back toward Clover Valley. They really needed to try to ditch the men long enough to make a plan.

"There's an abandoned mine shaft a little farther down the hill," she suggested. "It's under some boulders, so you can't see it from uphill. There's a decent chance they won't find us there."

He was silent, and she was sure the same thought that was going through her mind was going through his: what if their pursuers did find them? But that was a later problem.

Lightning flashed somewhere in the distance, lighting up the dark gray clouds. A rumble of thunder followed, and the rain that had fallen in slow drops in the forest was picking up, sounding a patter on her rain jacket and in the puddles in the path in front of her. Her coat and boots were keeping most of her dry, but the splatter of water hitting her jeans was starting to soak through.

Martin still hadn't responded to her suggestion, so she added, "We're really exposed out here. I don't know how long I can continue like this."

Her legs were losing their detached feeling, and she could feel herself slowing. The only thing saving her right now was going downhill. But to go to the next road, they would have to go back up. Paige knew this mountain like the back of her hand. That was their only hope, that they would find their way out of this mess faster than these men. She knew where to disappear, even if her endurance was low. She had to concentrate on that.

"Okay, we'll try the mine."

"They won't follow us. No one knows about this place, and hopefully the rain will cover our tracks," she said, then turned, picking up her pace again.

Paige and her sister had discovered the tunnels and explored them, despite their parents' warnings. There was an old No Trespassing sign that hung on one of the old support beams, but who could resist an old mining cave with planks that only half-blocked the entrance? It was a siren's call for two adventurous twelve-year-olds. One day when they'd slid through the rotting boards, they had heard the echo of footsteps deep within. She and her sister had tumbled out and ran behind the boulders that lined one side, whispering of tales of wild animals…until out came a girl with two bright pink braids.

"I heard you come in," she'd said with a sunny smile. "I'm Justine. You have to see what I found."

Justine was fun and independent in a way so foreign to the life that Paige lived. Plus, she was from San Francisco, equally interesting and foreign for the twins. Paige and Layla had never told their parents about their adventures with Justine exploring the mine, and now, as an adult, she could see all the dangers in this scenario, the kind that tweens didn't think about. Then came junior ski patrol and the Fabulous Five, and long summer afternoons with Justine and the mountainside faded.

It was strange that as they'd gotten older, her sister had held onto that sense of adventure, leaning into it, while Paige had moved away from it. Maybe it was that the world pushed them together so often that she'd felt an instinctive push to differentiate herself. So Layla had become the adventurous twin, and Paige had taken the safer road. She supposed that was just how things went with twins.

Today, Paige was making up for those years of lack of adventure. She just wished it didn't have to come on so suddenly.

"This way," she said pointing to a flash of light gray,

where the charred trees and mud stopped, and a jumble of boulders spread out that marked the top of the mine. As she followed the trail around the group of stones, familiar still after all these years, out of the corner of her eye she caught something fly through the air. Something black. It disappeared in a puddle somewhere downhill.

She whipped around. "What was that?"

"The gun I lifted from my attacker," he said. He threw a spray of dark pellets in the other direction off the trail. "And those were the bullets."

"Why did you do that?" she cried.

"My fath—" His voice was cut off as a flash of lightning blinded her, followed by a crash of thunder, so much closer. It rattled the ground, moving the mud under her feet, and she froze in place. The storm was heading for them, and on top of the pile of boulders, surrounded by the fire-swept mountainside, they were so exposed.

"We need to get to shelter," said Martin as another gust of wind whipped by.

She turned around, scanning as far as she could see, which wasn't a great distance. "I don't see the men, and I doubt they can hear us over the storm."

"Then let's go."

Or at least that was what she thought he'd said, but the wind carried his voice away. The skies opened up, and a downpour of thick drops pelted her face. The fog made it impossible to see more than a couple yards up the hill. The only thing good about their situation was that the men would have a harder time finding them. As she faced the path in front of her, she felt Martin's hand, gently lifting her hood.

"Thank you," she said. The gesture sent a burst of warmth

through her, and she tried to ignore the ache that followed. She missed being close to Martin.

Back in high school, there had always been something special about their friendship. Though Martin and Layla were more alike in many ways, more talkative, more likely to take charge of a situation, Paige had always felt a connection with Martin that went deeper. When Paige was around Layla at school, there were times she'd felt like the quieter, less interesting twin, but she'd never felt that way around Martin. Whether they were pairing off for lab partners in Chemistry or dividing up the slopes between the Fabulous Five team, she and Martin chose each other, time after time. Their complementary skills sets made the choice a logical one, but there had always been something more to it. Not quite romantic, just…right.

Paige never read into it any further until junior prom. The Fabulous Five had gone as a group, the way they did most things in those days. For dinner, Martin's father roasted ribs with his homemade barbecue sauce, and Juana's older sister, a pastry chef, made a custard tart topped with glazed strawberries, raspberries and kiwi, arranged so beautifully they had hesitated to cut into it. Benji's parents owned a limo service, so his father had driven the five of them in style.

Their class was small, and by the end of the evening, Paige had danced with just about everyone there. The whole night felt magical. Somehow, she and Martin had ended up together for the last dance, and it felt as if the party was coming to its natural end. But at some point during the dance, she'd looked up at Martin, and something shifted. It was as if she'd opened a door in her imagination, one that she'd never thought to try. That night, she'd turned the knob and revealed a new path, one where their friendship blossomed into something deeper.

Maybe it was the excitement of the evening, or maybe it was her family's moving date closing in on her, but for a few minutes under the flash of colored lights, she had met Martin's gaze and felt as if they were at the beginning of something beyond friendship. Even after all these years, she could still feel the gentle touch of Martin's hand on the small of her back that night, the way her breath caught in her throat when his dark eyes met hers, and he didn't look away. She could still picture the soft smile that had teased the corners of his mouth as he looked down at her while they swayed to the music.

At their dinner after their meetup in Sacramento, when Martin had met her gaze with the same soft smile she remembered so vividly, Paige's breath had caught in her throat, the same way it had all those years ago. Had she felt a new possibility of exploring that feeling, or had she just imagined it? When he ignored her calls and texts after, she'd decided the latter. But since he'd seen her across Main Street yesterday, he hadn't backed away, even when she'd given him opportunities. So were they back to being friends? She had to be careful not to read anything more into the way he was putting himself in danger to protect her.

She stepped into the next boulder in the pile, but her foot slipped from under her.

"Take my hand," Martin called from behind her, over the pelting of rain.

His grip was warm and strong, and they made their way down the mess of mud and charred wood, leaning on each other. The wind hit them head-on, whipping pellets of rain at her face.

"It's here, just below us," she said, pointing ahead at the ledge, barely visible through the gray.

Above, it didn't look like much of anything, just more

rocks on the uneven mountainside. Paige let go of Martin's hand and made her way around the rocky embankment, trying to ignore the way her anxiety stepped up a notch without the connection of his warm hand in hers. Together felt a lot better than doing this alone. She pushed that thought aside and focused on the boarded-up entrance to the mine shaft in front of her.

Back when they were kids, there had not been much to keep them out, so Paige and Layla had slipped between the boards and no one had known the difference. Now, someone had put up plywood that was still tan, not yet stripped of color by age and the sun, suggesting more recent efforts to board it up. But even more curious were the new support beams, reinforcing the entrance. One of the plywood boards was just leaning against the rest of them, not nailed tight. As she reached for the boards to pry them away, Martin held her back.

"Wait. Someone's been here."

Martin had always been good under pressure. Really good. It was what had drawn him to ski patrol rather than following in his mother's footsteps into the racing community, and it made him an excellent private investigator. He was methodical, able to weed out extraneous details and sort through the important elements, one by one, until he found the answer.

But right now, too many details surrounding them were far from extraneous. He and Paige were running from two men who had already proved themselves dangerous, and they were in the middle of a burn scar that was soaked with rain. Charred roots no longer held the mountain soil in place, and as soon as a deluge of water soaked the ground, gravity did its work, pulling the waterlogged mess down the mountain. He glanced out at the steep, now-barren mountainside. It was definitely mudslide territory. Next to him, he couldn't ignore how wet and afraid and still so resilient Paige was. When he looked at her, his heart seemed to squeeze in his chest, no matter how hard he tried to ignore it. She had spent just as much time on the mountain as he had when they grew up, both in the summers and in the winters. He shouldn't be any more worried about her out here than he was about himself. And yet, somehow, he was. But thinking about that right now was a distraction, exactly the kind that could put them in danger, so he blocked out the thought and focused on the footprints in the entrance of the mine shaft. Someone could be inside right now, and there was no reason to be inside this dark hole in the ground unless… He didn't even want to think about what that would be.

"Maybe those are my sister's prints," said Paige, staring at the mess of tracks on the ground. "She knows this place as well as I do. She went on foot because her truck is still at the cabin. This was the first place I thought to take refuge…"

Paige's voice faded as she looked up at him, her eyes alive with hope. It was a possibility, and not an unlikely one. Still, Martin shuddered at the thought of entering the mining tunnel. He preferred to move away from dark tight spaces, not toward them. But Paige needed a place to rest, and they were so exposed on the mountain. Without a clear plan for what to do, they needed a place to slow down and think through the next steps, so he tamped down those feelings. "Maybe, but would she stay here?" he asked.

"Only if she was in the same position as we are."

Martin had a bad feeling about this. Paige was staring at him with expectation written across her face, like she was waiting to burst through the loose board and run in. He checked his phone in hopes of finding a signal, but there was nothing. Paige must have known because she didn't bother to ask if he had one.

"I have to go in," she said. "If there's a chance my sister is there, I can't leave without checking."

They stood under the little ledge of the entrance to the mine shaft. There were what looked like old railroad ties that formed a sort of doorway. It was strange that some of the boards were new here. It was one thing to cover up the danger of the mine shaft opening—an owner trying to cover their liability in case someone wandered onto their property. But why reinforce the entrance…unless someone was using it. For what? The gold mines in this area had closed down a century ago or more when they were mined out.

"There are a lot of odd things about this situation," he muttered, as much to himself as to her.

She didn't answer, but her look told him everything. She was reminding him right now that this was her show. She was calling the shots. He didn't like the idea of going in there one bit, but if he refused, she'd go in alone.

Another flash of lightning lit up her face, and the rumble of the thunder came directly after, resonating through the mountainside. The thunder was rattling everything. The plywood board tottered, then fell toward them, and Paige's face lit up in alarm. "Was that an earthquake?"

"Too well-timed with the thunder for an earthquake," he said.

The thunderstorm wasn't their most urgent problem, so he turned to face the wooden plank propped against the side of the mine shaft.

"I'll move the plywood, and we can wait to see if there's any movement inside. The flashlight on my phone should give us a good view." At least his phone was good for something up here.

"Hopefully the boards rule out larger animals that might have wandered in," she said.

"Probably." Unless they were only recently put up. Martin really didn't want to accidentally corner a bear, a mountain lion or any of the other animals that roamed the area.

She gave him a wry smile. "When we were kids, I never once thought about those possibilities."

"I'm glad you never had to," he said. "If it seems okay, we'll slip in and close it up. That way if those two guys somehow follow us here, we'll have some warning when they open the plywood. It'll give us a few moments."

"This isn't visible from the main trail, and it's raining too hard to follow our footsteps."

"You're right," he said. "So if they find us here, it means they know about the mine shaft." He gestured to the newly closed up entrance. "Someone knows about it."

"What did my sister get into?" she whispered, and he was pretty sure she was asking the same questions and making the same connections he was.

The fear in her voice squeezed in his chest again. *Harden your heart.* The more involved he became, the harder it would be if they discovered something tragic. And if Paige asked him to ignore his code of ethics to put the safety of others first—including Paige's own safety—the way Presley had? Martin didn't want to think about that possibility. To get them out of this situation, he needed to keep his emotions and memories at bay.

"Let's stick with the immediate problem," he said gently.

She drew in a long inhale, then nodded. "Ready to go in?"

Not really, but he lifted the narrow piece of plywood and

moved it to the side. He stayed there for a moment, listening for movement, but the rain pounded hard on the heavy logs above him, drowning out any sounds from the cave. Another crash of thunder shook the world around them, and Paige tensed behind him. He turned on his flashlight and shined it inside. Definitely a mine that went deeper under the mountain, as promised, but he couldn't see anything that seemed out of the ordinary. He stepped in.

The tunnel was a long narrow shaft, just high enough for him to stand, and the walls were roughhewn, jagged from countless hours of labor with pickaxes. The sides and top were lined with rows of beams to stabilize the rock above them, but that was little comfort as far as Martin was concerned. Back in California history class, he'd read stories about the conditions of these mines, and it wasn't good. Martin wasn't particularly claustrophobic, but he didn't like the look of this dark passageway one bit. Paige had been in here many times, he reminded himself. He prayed it would hold up this time, too.

"Let's go," he said over his shoulder. "Stay quiet until we know more."

She nodded and slipped inside, and he followed, then put the board back in place. It was dark, lit only by the narrow beam of his phone and the thin cracks of daylight that glowed around the edges of the plywood. He closed his eyes to let them adjust, then opened them and moved the light around. The walls were a rainbow of gray and brown rock, glistening with moisture, and the floor was covered with rubble.

"Good news. No animals yet," he whispered.

"You always did look on the bright side," she said. He caught a hint of a smile.

But he didn't smile back. "That was a long time ago."

Was what she saw just her memories of him, or was that side of him still inside him somewhere?

At their dinner together a few months before, when it was just the two of them, he had felt the spark of his younger self rekindle. A lightness, and with it, a closeness he hadn't felt in years. The glow of their conversations and laughter had buoyed him on the car ride home, and as he crossed the Bay Bridge and the lights of San Francisco twinkled in the mist, he'd been tempted to call Paige, ask if she'd arrived home safely and float the idea of meeting again. He was still considering this possibility as he'd walked up the creaky wooden stairs to his flat. Could he still be the person she seemed to see in him? But when he opened the door and stepped into his dark apartment, that hope faded as the distress he'd seen too many times at his job came back. Whenever he thought about the endless clients in distress, he couldn't seem to shake the dampened pessimism that weighed on him.

Part of him wanted to explain all this to her right here, in this dark, damp cave. Part of him wanted to apologize for not calling her back. He hadn't responded because he'd been waiting for the right time to talk, when he was a little more ready to open up to her about work, about Presley… all of it. But the right time never seemed to come.

Maybe today there would be a chance. If they could find a moment when the list of threats wasn't quite as long.

"Can I call for my sister?" she asked. "In case she's somewhere down in the tunnels?"

He could hear a tinge of desperation in her voice, like she already knew the chances were small, but he nodded. "Better now, while we're close to the entrance."

"Layla?" Her voice echoed in the emptiness of the mine

shaft, bouncing off the glistening rock and returning to them. There was no reply.

"Layla?" she tried again. There was nothing. As they stood in the silence, she visibly deflated. It was as if she had put all her hopes on the idea that Layla was here, not letting herself think about other possibilities.

"We still need to check," she said softly. "If she's hurt, somewhere inside?"

"She's not here." Unless… Another possibility occurred to him, one that he didn't even want to entertain.

But she shook her head as if she had heard his thoughts. "She's alive. I know it."

Paige sounded surer than she had all day. The twins had always insisted on some sort of special communication between them, and he had never known quite what to make of it. Yet, she looked so much more hopeful, more determined than she had a moment before, so he nodded. Everything was better with a little hope.

"Those men think she is, too," she added. "They said something about a mutually beneficial agreement."

"Sounds like Layla has information they want to keep quiet."

Paige bit her lip. "She goes after corporations or institutions that abuse their power."

Martin nodded. "I read her stories on drug trafficking by prison wardens."

"She went into hiding for weeks after the story broke," she added.

"Tough job."

Paige frowned. "I'm just trying to figure out what it could be this time. We found that list of companies and property locations on the thumb drive… Maybe it's something about environmental hazards of a new development?

Maybe this is another story about the approval of housing projects built in fire territory? And we know people can go a long way when their financial reputation is on the line."

The shadows from his phone's flashlight highlighted worry lines creasing her forehead, and the raw vulnerability in her eyes scraped at him. He knew he should push that feeling away, focus on the immediate problems they were facing. Instead, he found himself resting his hand on her arm. She turned to look up at him, her dark eyes exposing the vulnerability hidden there, searching for comfort against the loneliness of fear. He knew better than to promise that it would be okay. All he could give her was support.

"I'm in this until we find Layla. We'll do this together."

"Thank you," she whispered, and for a moment he felt that burst of connection from their dinner, the one that somehow had been both a balm and an upheaval inside him. Now he felt it again, even stronger. *Together*. His own word rang inside him in a song of trust that made his heart skitter in his chest.

He looked away. This was the same trap he'd fallen into with Presley, making an investigation personal. The risk of things going wrong felt so much more weighted with Paige. She was one of his oldest friends, and he'd always cared about her.

"We need a plan for where to go next." Martin checked the reception on his cell phone once again out of habit, but it had no bars. "Where is the nearest place we can get help?"

"If we keep descending to the road below us, we can follow it to the subdivision a few miles up. Our friend's family has a cabin there…or at least she did." Paige's voice trailed off. Then she turned to Martin. "I have no idea if her family still owns the place, but Layla might try there."

Martin let out a sigh of relief. That plan sounded a lot

better than sticking around an empty mine shaft. "Let's find out. You ready?"

Before she could answer, a voice came through the boarded-up entrance.

"It's down here. I can see the entryway," said the unfamiliar male voice.

Martin froze, and his body tingled with fear. Their attackers had found the mine. He and Paige were trapped.

FIVE

Paige's heart exploded in her chest as she quietly backed away from the entrance. Martin switched off the flashlight from his phone, leaving them in the dim light from the entryway. Without the plywood on a sunny day, the cave lit up inside the mouth. That was where they had stayed when they were kids, a refuge from the sweltering heat that swept across the Sierra Nevada, just far enough to feed their imaginations. But right now, the dark skies cast an eerie glow where they stood. Paige glanced farther into the tunnel. There, the last of the light disappeared, leaving only darkness.

How had these men found them so quickly? It didn't make sense. When she and Martin had turned off the trail, no one was in sight. The entrance was easier to find from the road below, but only if a person knew where to stop, and on this stretch there were no turnoffs, just miles of burnt forest remains. So it made no sense that these men would somehow have followed them here. Unless they knew that the only place for shelter in this area was the mine shaft. They would also have to know the terrain well enough to find their way on forest markers alone.

Even knowing this, it would make more sense for them to head for the road and follow it to the nearest development a few miles away. And yet, they'd headed straight to the mine.

Who were they and why were they chasing Layla?

Lightning flashed again, and the entranceway glowed its terrible bright light, showing the silhouette of two men standing outside, just under the entrance of the mine shaft, but neither had made a move to enter. The thunder rattled the cave, worse than before, shaking the tunnel all around them. Dust and rocks fell from the ceiling, jolting her out of her confusion, and it seemed to do the same for Martin.

"We have no choice. We have to go farther in," he said.

Paige let out a shaky breath. As kids they had played "lost in the wilderness" countless times, imagining the creatures that lay deep within the dark mine while staying close enough to the front to escape. It had been part of the fun, to imagine bears hibernating inside, and every once in a while a skunk or a squirrel scurried out, frightening them.

Once on a dare, Paige had run to where the mine branched off into two tunnels. Both paths curved, and the last of the light disappeared. She'd touched the split, then sprinted back to the entrance to safety. Layla had given her front-seat privileges for a month after that dare, but Paige had paid for it with nightmares for months. Even now, she remembered the amorphous fear that seemed to linger in the darkness as she stumbled over loose rocks, desperate to get out.

When she'd brought up the idea of taking cover in the mine, she'd left out the details of her own fears because she hadn't thought they'd venture in this far. Now she had to face that darkness again, along with the crumbling of rocks around them. She knew they had no choice, that certain danger lay at the mouth of the cave, but her feet didn't want to move.

"We should try to get as far in as we can. Press yourself against the wall behind one of the wooden supports to hide," said Martin lowly. "If we can just get to the place where the tunnel splits, we'll be less visible."

She nodded and tried to keep her voice steady. "Be careful where you step. The rocks make a lot of noise."

"Let's go." Martin's voice was soft and so close, and he squeezed her hand. Paige closed her eyes, letting the warmth of his reassurance wash over her. She had deeply missed the way they could read each other, the way he seemed to know when she needed a boost of support and exactly how to give it. And now that she felt it again, she didn't want to lose it.

He let go, and she took a deep breath and forced herself to move deeper into the cave, placing each foot gingerly on the ground, testing for instability.

"They have to be in here" came the voice behind them, hesitant, and Paige had to wonder if they were approaching the cave with the same wariness she was. They were still lingering at the mouth. A flashlight sweeping in, and she leaped behind a thick log that held up the mine shaft, pressing herself against the wet rock.

"I don't see anyone," said another voice, and the light moved to the floor of the tunnel.

"Are you going to tell the boss we didn't check?" the first one asked.

Paige felt her way along the wet wall of the cave, trying not to kick stray rocks, or stray… No, she wasn't going to think about any other things, living or not, that were here. Martin went first, keeping his hand on the wall as he led them into the darkness. Paige's breaths were coming one on top of the other, echoing off the sides of the narrow tunnel. She tried to quiet them, but it was hard to control, especially with the snippets of the men's voices behind them, arguing as more thunder rumbled. A rock scraped under her foot, and she froze. Looked back. The two silhouettes were still in the same place, still facing each other, talking. Thank God.

Slowly, she made her way forward. More thunder rumbled, sending a new cascade of rocks and dust from the ceiling.

"This place is going to collapse." The voice echoed through the tunnel as they reached the fork.

"Which way?" Martin whispered.

"I've never been farther than this," she said.

"I can see why," he grumbled. "But as soon as we turn, we won't be visible from the entryway."

They turned down the side tunnel to the left, which was closer, plunging themselves into complete darkness.

"You go first." The voice of one of the men echoed in the tunnel. It was closer now, and the light flashed right where they had been standing just seconds before. The men had entered the cave, and they were coming straight for them. Her fear sent a cold spike through her. *Please, God, give me the strength to lead me through this.* She swallowed and reached out, grasping for Martin until she found his shoulder.

"Just making sure you're still here with me," she muttered.

"I'm here," he said, his low voice soothing. "I won't leave you."

There was a steadiness in his words, a promise that she had heard before when he insisted on going with her. How much did it take for him to keep up that strength? She didn't imagine he liked their circumstances any more than she did, but still he was by her side, offering her support.

Thank you, God, for bringing us together again.

A beam of light flashed behind them, hitting the end of the main tunnel. The men were coming for them. She shuffled forward, carefully treading over the rocks until Martin came to a standstill in front of her. If she weren't holding onto his shoulder, she would have bumped into him.

"There's something here," Martin said, his voice barely there over the mutters of the men behind them.

"What is it?" Her mind raced through the possibilities. A resting bear? A panther sleeping the day away?

The light flickered across the main tunnel behind them, and she strained to see what he was talking about, but all she saw was darkness.

"It's metal…some sort of machine? And it's blocking our way."

Again, Paige was thrown into a tumult of confusion. She didn't remember that much about the Gold Rush era, but she was pretty sure they'd used pickaxes, not machines. "Someone's definitely using this mine."

It was the only thing that made sense. This must be why the men had known about it. Now Paige was even more convinced that Layla had been here, and she must have discovered something about it—something that wasn't supposed to be found. Which meant they had stumbled into the last place they should have gone if they wanted to escape.

She shivered. Her damp jeans clung to her legs and rainwater that had seeped into her boots soaked her socked feet. They were venturing farther into the cold depths of the mountain, moving slower, and she could feel the cold seeping into her body. If she wasn't careful, she was going to get chilled. Badly.

"We should hide behind the machine and hope that the

men don't explore too deeply," said Martin, his voice barely audible.

She gave a murmur of agreement, and he started forward. With her other hand, she reached out and found the machine. It was about waist height, and the metal was cold and damp but smooth, without the corrosion of rust. It definitely hadn't been here since the Gold Rush. The machine had some sort of handle on one side, and the other was sharper. She flattened herself against the wall, making her way around it, keeping her hand on Martin's shoulder. He lowered himself so he was crouching behind the machine, and she followed. Martin's arm came around her shoulder, protective as he held her close. And she felt stronger. She wasn't in this alone, and she let herself be comforted by that, ignoring the wariness that followed, left over from after their Sacramento dinner.

The men's light flickered at the fork, and it flashed their way. Paige tried desperately not to move, not to breathe. She just prayed, reminding herself that she wasn't alone. But instead of lingering on the machine, the men focused the light on the ceiling.

"I'm not going in there," said the man. "Not with those bats."

Martin stiffened behind her, and Paige's breath caught in her throat. Bats? Her eyes flicked up to the ceiling, and there they were. Hundreds of small bodies, packed together. The bats clung to the rocks, but at the flash of light, she watched as they stirred. Moved their wings. Paige choked back a gasp. And then the light was gone, and the men flashed their light up the other tunnel.

She should have felt relief as their footsteps continued on, but she was frozen with fear. All she could think of was the bats hanging over them. Lightning flashed through the main tunnel, and thunder echoed, louder than before.

"We've got to get out of here," whispered Martin. "The men won't hear us with all the rocks falling."

"I guess that's one way to look on the bright side," she muttered.

Slowly, carefully, they moved out from behind the machine. She took Martin's shoulder and inched back toward the light, carefully weighing each step. She told herself that they hadn't disturbed the bats on their way in, so they just needed to be equally careful on the way out. It was the only thing that kept her from freezing up.

A new flash of lightning lit up the main tunnel, and thunder shook the mountain. But this time, it didn't stop. It rumbled, the sound growing until it felt as if the earth was moving all around them. Something was happening, something that vibrated through the mine shaft.

"Is the tunnel collapsing?" she gasped as dust and pebbles rained down on her head.

"Run," murmured Martin, grabbing her hand.

They took off toward the light at the entryway, their boots clacking over the loose rocks on the ground. Shouts came from the other part of the tunnel as they passed the fork their attackers had gone down.

"There they are!"

"Follow them!"

The men's words sent a chill down Paige's spine. She caught a glimpse of movement from the men's direction, and their voices were close—too close. She and Martin turned down the main shaft, and her boot slid out from under her. Paige stumbled, but Martin held her hand firmly, keeping her upright as she ran. They scrambled over the uneven ground. One of the men grunted out an obscenity behind them, and she forced herself not to turn and check how far away they were. The men were closing in on them. She could feel it. Her heart pounded in her chest, and her breaths were coming in short pants.

"Stop!" one of the men called.

Then a gunshot rang through the tunnel, deafening and final. Rock debris fell from the ceiling.

"What are you doing?" shouted the other man. "We need her alive."

Paige had barely registered that statement when the flap of wings and the screech of animals echoed through the cave. The bats. They were awake.

"Duck!" cried Paige, clutching her hood around her face as a colony of bats flooded the tunnel.

A swarm of bats flew everywhere around Martin, their wings brushing against his jacket, their flutters and chirps and squeaks sending shivers down his spine. Those sensations were all layered over the most distressing turn of events—nothing stood between the pursuers and Paige.

But Martin was good under pressure, or at least that was what he kept telling himself. Right now, he was starting to doubt that truth because the horde of bats flying all around him was too much. Except he couldn't let it be too much. Paige was here. And he had to protect her. So he blocked out the dark cave that was closing in around them, and he blocked out the bats that hit his back, and he focused on the one thing that mattered.

"Run!" he yelled, praying that the men behind him were just as thrown off by the bats as they were. "Just stay low and keep moving."

The men's shouts behind them were muffled, as if they, too, were struggling with the winged creatures and the falling debris. The animals' screeches were everywhere, but Paige's hand was a balm of reassurance as they stumbled toward the entrance of the mine. The bat horde was thicker there, the animals pouring out, but he held his hood against his face and forced himself through the opening as the creatures brushed against his back.

He took a sharp turn out into the rain again and then stumbled to a stop as he registered the changed landscape. It was as if the belly of the mountain had been split, and all of its guts had oozed out, exposing its insides. While they were underground, the storm had displaced everything, creating chaos. It looked like a slow-moving river of mud, rocks, uprooted plants, and the trunks of trees, charred from last summer's rain fires, still helplessly clinging to their roots. The boulders that surrounded the mine had kept the worst at bay, and for that he was thankful. Without them as barriers, the mud would have poured over the entrance, blocking it.

Or it would have collapsed.

"A mudslide," called Paige. "That was the big shaking sound we heard."

After so much rain, the soil had finally reached its saturation point, and without the roots of the plants to keep it in place, it had all let go. The mudslide had pulled everything down the mountain. Where there used to be paths, there was now a thick mess of mud and debris. What was worse, the rain hadn't stopped. The ground was no more stable than it had been before. The moment they set out across it, there was a chance of another slide, a chance that they would be stuck, even buried, in it. But they didn't have a choice. The threat behind them was still worse.

Today really wasn't Martin's day. After nearly being shot right outside Paige's cabin, he'd forced himself to run into the open scorched landscape, then into—not away from—the cramped tunnel of the mine shaft. They'd escaped a colony of bats only to find themselves in this unrecognizable landscape. For Paige, it was even worse. Because on top of everything they'd been through, her twin sister was still missing.

"We have to keep going," said Paige.

They needed a place to hide. The men would be exiting the cave any minute, as soon as they got themselves through the stream of bats that were still pouring out of the entrance. But Martin heard a plea in Paige's voice, too, as if she was fighting some internal argument. Was she fighting exhaustion or the overwhelming urge to resign herself to defeat? If she was, Martin knew Paige would never give up, no matter how hard things got. He had always admired that about her. From the time they had dug someone out of an avalanche on a search and rescue mission as teens, when a fun job had suddenly turned much more serious, he knew where her heart was. When someone was in need, she would be there—even at the risk of her own safety. This was what worried him the most. It was also why he was absolutely certain that she was not going to give up on finding her sister.

Raindrops splattered his face, and he gazed out at the dark landscape, enshrouded in rain clouds. "We need to climb the embankment and find a way back to the stable ground."

She shivered. "But we don't know how far this slide goes."

"Then we need to keep running."

She met his gaze, and the trust he saw made his breath catch. *Please give me the strength to live up to her trust.* The prayer flowed from deep inside, surprising him. It had been so long he had thought this part of him had disappeared. But he didn't have time to contemplate this right now. He had no idea how much time they had to escape, but all they could do was hope and run. And pray.

"You first," he said. If she fell, he wanted to be there for her.

She grabbed hold of the rocks and hoisted herself up the embankment, slipping through the new mud. He followed her, moving quickly away from the mouth of the mine shaft. By the time he reached the top, the mud had seeped over the ankles of his boots.

Martin squinted through the rain, but the landscape disappeared into the fog and darkness. Lightning flashed, a sharp, jagged line from the sky to the mountain and for a moment he thought he spotted a tree line, somewhere in the distance. Could they make it through this?

The thunder shook the ground, and Paige whispered next to him, "Let's go. I think I saw the trees."

Good. She'd seen it, too. They started at an angle down the steep decline, around boulders and through the mud-covered branches. Paige's breathing was fast, faster than his own. Faint sounds of voices echoed behind them through the rain, and as he climbed over a mud-drenched tree trunk, Martin glanced over his shoulder. The two men had finally escaped the bats and were standing on the ledge, gesturing in their direction.

"The men are close behind," he said, hoping it would help them both find the extra reserves of energy. At some point, everyone's body gave out, no matter how determined they were to keep going.

He waited for more gunshots, but they didn't come. While he was expendable to these men, Paige was not… at least until they had Layla and figured out Paige knew nothing, he suspected. He followed in Paige's path, trudging through the mud. When he turned around again, a thick fog had enveloped the mine. Paige made her way over the wreckage of the landscape, testing logs and boulders before she moved around them. The steep mountainside could move under their feet at any minute. He scanned to look through the mist until the darkness of the forest grew clearer. And then he could see a utility pole. The utility lines that climbed the mountain marked a break in the forest, and judging from the treetops coming into sight, the path cleared for these lines seemed to have served as a fire line, which now separated the charred, muddy mountainside from the still-green forest. Once they reached the forest, they could find somewhere to hide. Thank God.

Paige turned, looking into the mist behind them. Then she rested her palms on her knees, and her back rose and fell like she was heaving in deep breaths.

"You okay?" he whispered.

She nodded.

"We have to keep going."

She nodded again and continued with heavy steps. Her cheeks were flushed, and her hair was plastered to the side of her face. He caught a snippet of a voice floating through the rain and wind, and Martin didn't want to think about how close the men were. His and Paige's only hope was to find a place to hide and pray that they wouldn't be seen.

Martin walked by Paige's side, stealing glances, trying to gauge how much more she could endure. Her slowing steps told him that her energy was waning, but when she looked up and met his gaze, the determination in her eyes was not. In this moment, he could see how far she would push herself, no matter how much her body needed a rest. This was for her sister, and she would never abandon Layla. Even at the cost of herself. Even though this drive scared him, he also admired her protective instincts. Paige's love for her sister was a source of deep strength, and as he watched her, a mix of respect and warmth buoyed him.

She looked at the ground again, and Martin saw her lips moving, as if she was praying. Somewhere deep inside him, he could feel her distress resonating through her, and it threatened to break the dam of all the unwanted feelings that he was so carefully holding at bay. He had suppressed this sensation so many times, shoved his feelings deep down inside him as he witnessed the distress of the people he was helping. He told himself he could ignore this heaviness inside him for just one more job. Except this was Paige, and it didn't feel anything like a job. When this was over, he promised himself he'd figure out what to do about this. For now, he needed to focus on protecting her from the people who were chasing them, but he also needed to protect her from collapse.

As much as Martin would prefer to get much more distance from these men before they rested, he knew they needed to stop. Just a little rest would help.

"We should find somewhere to take shelter," he said.

She looked like she was going to argue, like she was going to tell him that they couldn't stop. He could see the fear in her expression, the drive to help Layla. But she was panting so quickly, and she had to slow her breathing to even speak. She closed her eyes, and finally she nodded.

"Okay. But just for a moment," she said.

He looked down the utility clearing. "Let's get out of the open area."

Paige scanned the landscape. "We're close to a place where we can hide, but it's not out of the rain."

They climbed out of the mudslide and into the scrubby terrain of bushes and green sprouts peeking up from the ground. Lightning flashed, and as he turned, two figures lit up on the mountainside. A chill of fear ran through him. The men were catching up. If he and Paige didn't move faster, they wouldn't have the chance to hide.

The rain pattered the canopy of trees above as they moved through the woods. The ground was stable here, and Paige moved faster, sidestepping bushes, following one path, then another. They came to a group of boulders, and she pointed to a crevasse. "If we slip between these two rocks, there's a space, like a cave without a top."

Then she froze, and he did, too. Voices, even closer this time. Paige shivered, and he wasn't sure if it was from the cold or from the fear or both. He wanted to put his arm around her, to comfort her, but instead he gestured toward the opening where she'd pointed. She climbed down into the crevasse, descending, and he followed. It was narrow, better sized for kids than adults, and as he squeezed through the opening, he hoped it meant these men wouldn't think to check inside it. It helped him not think about the possibility of getting stuck. His jacket dragged along the granite wall. As he stepped down a sharp slope, a clearing came into sight. It was small with tall sheer rock slabs as its walls. He could see why Paige and Layla might have loved to escape into this spot when they were younger, but in this situation, it had a major downside: there was no other escape route. If the men checked this spot, they were trapped. Again.

He squeezed through the last inches and found Paige sitting on a stone outcrop. She was hunched over, hugging her knees. She looked so scared and alone, clearly so worried for her missing sister, and the pain of seeing her like this was just too much. The weight of the last few years hit him hard. He had reunited runaway teens with desperate parents and lost siblings with each other. But more often, the ending came to nothing good. And in those moments he'd seen the pain, it felt as if he was viewing the grand injustices of the world.

Presley and his family had put Martin in the tough position of personal loyalty versus what he thought was right when they'd subtly threatened his reputation if he did anything to reveal the brother's location. Martin had ignored their warnings and called social services. The family had followed through on their threats, and Martin had taken a hit for it. If he hadn't worked for his uncle, who was already well-established and trusted in the area, the family's efforts would have been even worse.

But even before that case, there had been other cases that had shaken him. The disappearances were the hardest. The families were so hopeful when they learned that most people who disappeared were found, but too often, finding the person didn't bring the relief that they'd hoped for. He always came back to Marina, a middle-aged mother of two young kids whose husband disappeared shortly after their wedding. Martin had found the husband…who had been arrested and jailed for possession of huge amounts of prescription drugs. The husband hadn't planned to tell Marina about the arrest, figuring he'd be released soon enough and just say he lost his phone. If Martin had been any slower at tracking him down, the guy would have been released, and Marina would never have known the difference. It was only because Marina had the money to hire a private investigator that she found out about her husband's drug habit and his way of financing it: selling the same prescription drugs he used to others.

He'd started to fear what might happen to the people he loved, that they'd be in Marina's situation—that they'd discover a secret about someone closest to them, a secret that would tear their lives apart—so he had withdrawn, pulled away from his family and friends, just to try to stop these feelings. But right now, they wouldn't stop. What if something had happened to Layla, something that would wreck Paige? It would take him down, too.

If he had been anywhere else, with anyone else, he would've made an excuse and left. Found a way to build up his defenses again before he continued. But he was here, trapped on the mountainside, unable to turn away. And the men hunting them were right on their tail.

SIX

Paige crouched on the cold wet stone, making herself as small as possible, trying to keep her heaving breaths soundless. Martin was crouched next to her, still and on high alert. It took all her energy not to pant, not to gulp in air. Her body still wanted to flee, that nervous fear coursing through her, begging her to find her sister.

Logically, she knew her legs would give in soon. She had been ignoring the rubbery feeling for far too long. She knew this about herself from their search and rescue missions, that in crisis situations, she didn't register the cues that her body was on the brink of collapse—not until she was on her knees. Paige had learned how to deal with this, how to pace herself, when to force herself to stop, to eat, to drink, to take a moment and listen to the rate of her heartbeat, the sound of her breaths. It had been so long since she'd had to remember this, since she had brought herself this close to collapse. If Martin hadn't been here... No. She wasn't going to think about that possibility. Because he *was* here, and he had somehow understood that she needed to stop, regardless of the fact that her brain was telling her to keep going.

"They can't get far on foot," said a voice through the

rain. "If we can get service, we can call the others to head them off."

The others. There were definitely more men out there. At least two others, if she counted the driver of the van as one. Her mind traveled back to the van, the panic as the man pulled her closer to the open door…

As the rain beat down on her head, her brain worked overtime, coming up with every worst-case scenario, urging her to help her sister before it was too late. But the men's voices traveled through the fog, so close, so she did the only thing she could think of to control this feeling. *Please, Lord, keep her safe. I know she's somewhere out there alive. And I can feel her distress. Please, Lord. If she is alone, comfort her.*

The men's voices broke through her prayers.

"Where else could they go?" said the other man. "It's… to town…closer…fancy development…"

She only caught a few words, but they made her blood run cold. Were those men heading for the lake where Justine's family had a cabin, just like she was planning to? Their friend's "cabin" was one of those fancy places, the kind where people came for the weekend and then left. Layla would think it was the perfect place to hide, especially since no one but Paige knew about their connection. Now it sounded like these men were looking in the subdivision, assuming Paige and Martin were headed there. Was Layla still in touch with Justine? If Justine's family was there and Layla showed up, everyone in the house was in danger.

The thoughts rattled through her head, and then through her body, awakening new rushes of fear. Was she bringing danger toward her sister instead of helping? Paige's legs shook with fear, aching to react. She balled her hands into fists, forcing herself to stay still.

She tried to blocked out the voices of the men that were fading into the forest. She told herself that she and Martin had been trapped in the mine shaft and managed to make it out. She had kept herself together through the flurry of bats that encircled them, their fluttering wings pelting her back. She could make it through this, too. With Martin by her side, she would find her sister. No matter what.

Martin's movement caught her eye. Slowly, so slowly as to avoid the scrape of his jacket against the boulders, he placed his warm hand on hers. Her breathing stuttered, and without warning, she felt the tears well as she unclenched her fist and took his hand. It was too much to turn, to risk the movement of her hood and her jacket, the scrape against the rock, so she simply closed her eyes and let the warmth of his hand comfort her.

"Thank you," she whispered, and she felt the depth of her gratitude flow through her. He was here for her, really here for her. Despite the fact that he had ignored her after their dinner together.

"I thank God for bringing us together," she added, almost to herself, as she focused on the sound and the feeling of her breaths slowing.

Martin gave her hand a squeeze, then let go. He gave her a tight smile. "I don't know what to think of God these days."

She studied his deep brown eyes, waiting for him to continue, but he seemed to pull away, just when it felt as though he was opening up.

Why did she have to keep reminding herself not to fall for him? Now, while she was feeling so vulnerable from Layla's disappearance, she took so much comfort in the closeness that had been blooming between them. There was so much about him she loved. Paige tensed as the word *love* floated through her mind. She couldn't think of this as more than friendship when he was so clearly setting limits.

Finally, he looked at the ground and gave a little laugh. "I haven't prayed this much in years."

"Fear has a funny way of returning us to God," she said, then gave him a wry smile. "That's my attempt to look at the bright side of things."

He smiled at her, but there was something more in his expression, something she couldn't read. A bolt of lightning lit the cave, and he reached for her hand again and squeezed it gently as the thunder rumbled.

She squeezed back and reminded herself that she wasn't alone. Then he glanced down at their hands, intertwined, and a strange look crossed his face. It was gone almost instantly, and he let go of her and wiped some of the rain from his face.

Paige swallowed. She had to let this topic be and focus on finding Layla.

"If Layla is at our friend's house, those men are heading straight for her," she whispered.

Martin nodded, but he didn't move to get up.

"If we're going to continue, we need to eat," he said. *I'm going to take care of you if you won't take care of yourself*, his expression seemed to say. Totally what friends did for each other. And despite the fear and exhaustion and the worry that was coursing through her, she felt the corners of her mouth kick up.

"Is that a suggestion, or are you putting your foot down?"

A sparkle of humor lit his smile. "I'm hoping it'll just stay as a suggestion."

"What do you have?"

He unzipped the pocket of his dark gray jacket and pulled out two energy bars and a plastic baggie of brown pellet-like bits.

She pushed back her hood, letting the rain hit her face. "Those look like dog treats."

He beamed at her. "You're right. My homemade specialty, the kind no dog can resist. You never know when you'll need them. They've saved me before."

"So you cook these days?"

He gave her a hint of a smile. "When properly motivated."

"I'm intrigued, but I'll start with an energy bar," she said.

Paige caught sight of her hands smeared with dirt. Sticking them out in the rain, she let the drops fill her palms. She rubbed them together, then wiped them on her wet jeans. When they approached clean, he handed her a bar. Their fingers brushed as she took it, and her heart kicked up in a more-than-friends way. Which Paige did her best to ignore.

She opened the energy bar carefully and took a bite, then let out a sigh of relief. "Never have these tasted better."

"You said that more than once, when we were up on the mountain back in high school," he said.

"And I meant it every single time." She smiled at him, and when he smiled back, it felt so easy between them. And yet there were these moments when he seemed to close down and pull away. She wanted to understand what he'd meant by his comment about God earlier. "What did you mean before when you said you didn't know what to think about God these days?"

Martin frowned, and for a moment she thought he wasn't going to answer. He glanced at her, his expression a little wary. "My job has made it tough to see the brighter side of life. And that includes keeping up my faith."

There was a heaviness in his voice she'd heard hints

of these last two days, but now she felt the full force of it. Something squeezed inside her chest as she heard how much this weighed on him. She reached for his hand, the hand that had comforted her more than once over the last day. She prayed she could give him even a fraction of the comfort he had given her. "I'm so sorry, Martin."

He met her gaze and nodded, and the squeeze in her chest lifted a little.

"I imagine you see things that make life look pretty bleak," she said, gently prompting him, hoping he'd say more. Layla had said something similar in the past, when she was working on the story about prison wardens, and what her sister had needed most was to talk to someone who would listen without judgement. Maybe Martin needed the same.

He studied her for a moment, and she got the feeling he was deciding whether to say more. His eyes softened, and he said, "There is just so much suffering out there. Seeing it firsthand, day after day, wears on me, and I feel this distance…to others, to God."

She nodded. He was quiet for a while, still watching her. Then he gave her a quick smile. "I didn't want to bring this up when we had dinner in Sacramento. It felt so good to talk to you again, and I didn't want to ruin it."

Paige shook her head. "Talking about hard things wouldn't ruin a dinner for me."

"Then maybe we'll need to try again," he said, flashing her a wry smile.

"Definitely," she said, feeling a burst of hope, then the doubt that so quickly crept in. Would he return her calls this time…or would he shut her out again?

They were quiet, and Martin frowned. "You think those men are heading to where you hope Layla is hiding?"

Paige swallowed. "If the others aren't already there. Which is why we need to hurry to warn her. Because now they probably will guess that I am heading in that direction to meet up with Layla." Which meant she had inadvertently put her sister into new danger.

Martin shook his head. "Don't go down that road, Paige. You're not responsible for other people's bad behavior."

Logically, she knew this, but she couldn't help thinking, what if she hadn't been there? Would Layla have been safer on her own?

Martin tried to keep his focus on the present. Each time the conversation waned, Paige looked tired and worried, and they were so far from out of danger. Still, as he sat there, crouched behind the stone, staring at the overly sweet and vaguely strange-tasting energy bar, his mind kept drifting back to the moment just a few minutes ago, when she'd asked him about his faith. There had been a strange relief in confessing.

His hand had brushed against hers, and something about it had felt different.

It shouldn't have felt different. They'd held hands today, an old habit back from search and rescue, when things got dangerous on the mountainside. Their junior ski patrol leader had used this as a way to connect to the group, whether that was with hands or ropes or anything, as a big boost of safety and morale.

But somehow, as they crouched against the cold rocks, with the rain soaking through his jeans and their two pursuers lurking somewhere on the mountain, this touch had felt different. Something had shifted in him when he'd started to talk about the distance and isolation he'd experienced these last few years. He'd felt a rush of relief when her expression had opened, not closed, and her eyes were filled with acceptance. Now, his heart refused to harden, and instead, it felt as if it had opened to new possibilities, the kind that had floated between them that night at dinner in Sacramento, just the two of them. The kind he knew so well not to entertain. Because behind the hope that fluttered inside him, there was a fear of loss lingering, one that hurt just to think about.

Martin didn't know what to do with these thoughts. Maybe he should just write them off as what it meant to care deeply for his friends. After being through some of the most harrowing risks together as a teenager, perhaps the bond hadn't weakened, even after years of distance. It just felt so good to see her again, to have this part of him, a part that had been dormant for years, come alive again. He had felt this way at dinner in Sacramento, and it was intense enough to make him pull away afterward. Now that feeling was more intense and, therefore, more painful.

Focus.

"How's your energy level?" he asked. It was amazing that he sounded so normal despite the shock of his own revelation.

"Honestly, I have no idea," she said, giving him a hint of a wry smile. "But I'm ready to go."

"You want to follow those men?"

"Up the road a few miles, there's a turn off into the Lakewood Estates subdivision. Basically, it's a bunch of upscale houses built around a human-made lake. They plopped it down right in the middle of the forest."

"The one that was delayed because people thought it was a major wildfire hazard?" he said.

"Well, they were right. They think last summer's fire was sparked from a bonfire at one of the places."

Martin let out a low whistle.

"Grandma hated that subdivision," she continued, "so we never actually told her that we had a friend who lived there." Paige let out a little laugh. "It's why Layla would think this was a great hiding place. Because I'm the only other person who knows about this connection."

Following their pursuers sounded like a very bad idea, one he knew he wasn't going to be able to talk her out of. He considered the angles, one by one, until he came up with a new possibility. "A place like that, you think they'd have cell phone service, right?"

She considered it, then nodded. "Most of those people would want the internet at the very least. So if they don't have service, maybe we can use someone's Wi-Fi to call for help?"

"We can head in that direction," he said, considering his words carefully, "but we shouldn't do anything on our own if there's a chance we can get help. You know that as well as I do."

There was no way Paige had forgotten this part of their training. How many rescues had they done because someone had attempted something on their own? How many times had Paige heard victims say, *if only I had taken a buddy with me...*? And yet today, she had been willing to go out on her own to try to find her sister, despite the fact that she had always been the most cautious of their group. He didn't have to point out any of this directly because he could see she had drawn the same conclusions. What if she had gone to her grandmother's cabin by herself? Would she have been caught by those men?

The thought sent an icy tingle down his spine, so he pushed it away.

"You're right," she finally muttered. "I know you're right."

"And we both know how hard it is to think through these things in the middle of a crisis," he added gently.

She pushed up to standing, and he did, too.

"What about the mudslide? How can we get help if it crossed the road?" she asked.

"We need to check that out. I know you want to hurry to find your sister, but it's better if we make sure to stay a little behind the ones chasing her, far out of sight. We have no idea where they are."

SEVEN

Paige made her way downhill along the trail of pine fronds and mud, hopping over gullies of runoff from the beating rain. The road wasn't far, but the fog was too heavy for a view of anything more than the forest in front of her.

Walking in muddy boots and wet jeans wasn't ideal. But then, nothing about this situation was ideal… Nothing aside from having Martin here with her. She had lost track of how many times she had thanked God that he was here by her side. He still seemed to know her, to understand her just as well as he had back in high school. Or, strangely, maybe he even knew her better now. That evening in Sacramento, when she had confessed that she loved eldercare but wanted something a little more fast-paced, he'd said, "You always loved getting dragged into more adventure than you would have chosen yourself." This was exactly the struggle she'd been trying to put her finger on for the last year, and he'd understood it immediately. It was as if their relationship had picked up exactly where it had been and then grown to fit their lives today. Now, over the course of the day, it had deepened again. The thought lifted her as they made their way toward the roadside, listening for voices or traffic over the rain.

If a stray car drove by, maybe they could hitch a ride

back to Clover Valley…but that would mean leaving Layla behind for now. The thought didn't sit well with her. But if the mudslide covered the road, it would block the only direct route into town, which meant a fiftyish mile loop downhill, then back up. It would mean they were all stuck here together—her, Martin and possibly Layla but also the men who were hunting them. And whatever unfortunate residents were spending this stormy day in their lakeside homes. She ruled out heading back up the mountain for Martin's car and drive back into town for more help, at least for now. It would take too long to work their way uphill again, and there wasn't a good way from that road to get back to the subdivision. Which would mean she wouldn't be able to get to Layla for hours. They didn't have that kind of time to spare.

Finally, the road came into sight, the flat strip of asphalt below a wall of mountain. They were perched a few yards up, on top of the granite rock that had been sheared long ago to make way for the road. They needed to find a path down.

They followed the ledge, rounding the bend in the road, until a mess of mud, rocks and branches spread out in front of them. Through the mist, Paige traced the mudslide as it funneled into the gulch, then spilled its guts into the road. The route to town was completely blocked. Even if they crossed the mudslide and hiked the ten-plus miles back toward town, they wouldn't be able to make their way to the subdivision for hours and hours, too long to leave Layla out on her own.

The slope of the mountain was steeper here, and she clung to rocks and tree trunks as she picked her way down to the buried road. Martin ventured onto the street as she studied the edges of the mudslide.

"No footprints that I can see, so chances are our attackers didn't take this path," he called.

"But maybe an animal." She pointed to vague indents in the mud.

"What kinds of wildlife roam around here these days?" he asked, then gave her a dry smile. "Besides bats."

She shivered at the memory. "There are still hungry bears that roam around in the spring, looking for food. That hasn't changed. Most people are better about bear-proofing their trash these days, but it's always a risk."

He nodded.

"Then there's the packs of wild boars that tear through the area," she added. "They leave trampled paths wherever they've been. I think we'd see a lot more prints if the boars had been here. I also saw a bobcat outside the cabin last summer. I've heard mountain lions and panthers are still around here, but I haven't seen any. Probably because I try to avoid wandering around at night."

"Wise plan," he said.

"Are you assessing our danger level?" she asked, and she felt the corners of her mouth lift. It was the kind of thing he used to do on ski patrol.

"Always."

Her smile faded as her thoughts returned to Layla. "Let's start toward the subdivision."

Her legs felt a lot less shaky now that the energy bar was hitting her system, but she was dying for a glass of water. As they made their way uphill, along the road, she promised herself she'd rest and take care of herself. Soon. Once she made sure her sister was out of danger.

If this were a regular job, Martin would have welcomed the silence as they made their way along the two-lane road.

He could listen for noises, conserve energy. But so much about energy levels and quick thinking was mindset, especially in a crisis. And as soon as Paige went quiet, her brow furrowed, he was almost sure her worries were taking over. It was hard to watch Paige struggle, hard to know she was feeling pain. Martin searched his mind for something to talk about, something that would distract her.

But what could he ask about? She had updated him about her job and her current life in Clover Valley at dinner. But he hadn't asked what it was like for her when she left their hometown.

"Tell me more about New Mexico," he said, keeping his voice low under the patter of the rain. "It seems like you and Layla had a good senior year."

Paige shrugged. "We did, I suppose. That's one of the benefits of having a twin. We weren't alone, and that eased some of my anxiety about a new school. We were the brand-new Californians and it was a small town so...people were interested in us."

She glanced over at him and then added, "But it never really felt like home. We missed being part of the Fabulous Five. A lot."

Her voice was quiet, and he felt a stab of guilt looking back at his former self, so careless about staying in touch. Liking or commenting on someone's social media wasn't the same as staying in contact. And though he had missed them, he hadn't quite known what to do about it. In those early days, calls and group text didn't make up for the distance. Their Fabulous Five group had broken up.

But now that nine years had passed, he could see this from Paige's point of view, too. They had lost everything familiar, and not by choice. No matter how hard it was for him when they left and their group became disjointed, losing touch in an unfamiliar place would have been even more difficult for her.

"Things weren't the same without you," said Martin, though he knew it wasn't enough. He, Juana and Benji had spoken these words over the years, but Paige and Layla probably never really understood how much they meant it.

"I'm glad things weren't the same when two of your friends disappeared," she said in that teasing voice he remembered so well, but he could hear that there was hurt buried somewhere in there, too.

"It was hard, really hard. They placed two new people on our patrol team. Perfectly fine but younger, just starting out and… It wasn't the same," he said, and there was an intensity to his voice that surprised him. "Nothing was the same."

I still miss having you in my life. Martin didn't know why he held that last part back. He wasn't sure what to make of it, the intensity of that thought and how during his senior year, he had simply tried to block it out. He hadn't been much more introspective than the average teenage boy at the time. That came later, with his job. But right now, those moments came back, when he'd see a picture of Paige on some social media post and look away, distract himself with something else.

That feeling of loss, that helplessness to change the situation had been one of the reasons he had gone into his uncle's private investigation business. If that absence had caused him so much ache, what was it like for the people who had no way of knowing what had happened to their loved ones?

Loved ones. He told himself the words resonated because he loved his friends. He told himself there was no reason those words should feel a little unsettling and ignored the unease that churned inside him.

"You seemed to enjoy San Francisco State," she said.

"It was a big change, and I guess I wasn't expecting it to be like that," he said. "Even though, growing up, I'd spent a lot of time at my grandparents' place in Oakland, I wasn't prepared for how different it would feel to actually live in a city."

He gave a little laugh as he remembered himself after the first few weeks away from the mountains. "I felt a level of comfort being around people from all over the world and hearing different languages when I walked down the street. But I couldn't get used to the constant noise. I spent a lot of weekends at my parents' place that first year. But I got used to it and now it feels like home."

"No plans to take over Hosey's Outdoor Adventure Sports?" she asked.

He smiled. "Someday. I know they'd love me to, but my dad wants to make sure that I really want it."

His parents had wanted him to go off and live his own life before deciding what to do about the store, and after senior year, when Paige and Layla left, he had understood that everything would change, that the life he had in Clover Valley wasn't going to be the same as it always had been if he stayed.

Moving back to his hometown was something Martin hadn't thought about in a while. But despite the reasons why he and Paige were together right now, he couldn't deny how good this felt, to be on home territory with her.

"How come you never called when you visited your parents these last few years?"

The question surprised him. He shrugged, not sure what to say. He glanced at her and caught her flushed face turning brighter.

"I messaged you twice after our dinner in Sacramento. And called." She looked away, into the darkening forest.

Martin still didn't know how to explain it, especially now that walking next to her felt so natural. But after the last few years of the distance he'd felt when friends and colleagues talked about their work and relationships with so much warmth, he'd started to feel like something was just…missing from his life. And he hadn't figured out how to tell her this. He'd told her about the emptiness he'd felt back on the mountain, but bringing it up again now would probably sound like an excuse.

"I'm sorry. I should have responded," he said, because that was all he really could say.

She flashed him an unexpected smile. "Forgiven. Besides, you're more than making it up to me right now."

He shook his head. "When this is over, I want to go to dinner again. My treat."

She glanced at him with a look he couldn't read.

"That's what a real friend would do," he added.

"Okay," she said, but she still sounded wary.

It was a reminder to focus on the friendship they were rekindling, not the complicated feelings that would have the power to disturb their tentative reunion. He wasn't going to harden his heart from her pain—that much was becoming clear. But he wasn't going to jeopardize their renewed connection with that strange mix of closeness and fear he had felt when he'd confessed his doubts back on the mountainside, either.

As they neared Lakewood Estates, Paige signaled to move downhill, into the ditch. They both fell silent, listening. The rain from the trees spilled in deluges every time the wind blew. The forest was far from quiet. It covered their own sounds, which she was grateful for, but it also meant that the men who were looking for them would be hard to detect by sound. Somewhere inside her, Paige could feel how tired she was, but her mind was far from stopping. It was as if her body was trying to turn off its signals, disconnect so that she could push on. She would give out at some point, but not yet.

"The subdivision is coming around the next bend," said Paige in a low voice. "We should probably go farther into the forest."

She led the way around raggedy shrubs, keeping the road above them in sight. As they rounded the curve, the green of the well-watered lawns came into sight—a rarity in these parts, too often parched during the rainless summers to sustain grass. This patch of manicured grass was situated on a gentler slope, and in the middle was a sign, built of brick and stone, with the words Lakewood Estates etched in cursive on it. Between her and the sign was a road into the subdivision, newly asphalted, though the water from the rains had already started to do its work, loosening it from underneath and splitting it apart. The homeowners' association would likely just pave it over, and then it would crack again in that unending cycle of reclaiming that the natural world never tired of. That was what her grandmother would've said about it, if she had been here and not in the home that her parents had bought for the family in the New Mexico desert. Her grandmother's arthritis was much better, but every time Paige talked to her, she could hear how much her grandmother missed the woods. And every time, Paige promised not to change the place, not to bring in new "modernizations," not to make it into something that her grandmother never wanted it to be.

They walked silently down the hill until they found a trail not far from the road.

"What kind of animal do you think made this trail?" Martin whispered.

"Probably deer," she said, then glanced over her shoulder. "Maybe with the help of mountain lions."

"Let's hope not," he mumbled.

Still, those animals sounded less threatening than facing the men who were after them.

EIGHT

Martin gazed up ahead, between them and the road, where the forest had been cleared. The worries about fire had grown in the experiences and imaginations of the people in the Sierra Nevada, and there was more and more effort to figure out how to not let a wildfire sweep through again. Maybe it was guilt from last summer, and maybe it was just a deep-seated reality setting in—that fire made its own way, its own path, and it was much too powerful for humans to control.

He pointed to a pile of felled logs off to the side where they could stop and assess their next move. They would search her friend's home for Layla, but at any sign of trouble, he wanted to get Paige out and call for help. They climbed up the hill, and the wet ground sunk under his feet as he squatted behind the log pile at the top. From there, he peered to look through the trees, into the subdivision that lay lower down the mountain. Daylight was fading, the gray rain clouds darkening. Through the woods and down the hill, he could see the twinkling of lights shine through.

"This is it," she said.

Martin turned to her, giving her a hint of a smile. "At least it's not uphill from here."

"Always looking on the bright side," she said, shaking her head.

This time, he didn't frown at the memory of their past life.

Paige studied downhill as he scanned the area around them. Nothing out of the ordinary.

"Those men seemed familiar with the cave, and we found that machine at the end of the tunnel," she said, looking out into the distance. "That doesn't point to a new development. So who are they? What could they want from an abandoned mine?"

"Your sister is a naturally curious person…" he started.

She gave a quiet snort of laughter. "That's an understatement."

"What if the story she's persuing started when she stumbled onto something on the parcel next to your grandmother's, something to do with the mine?"

Paige furrowed her brow. "It's possible. But who would they be?"

"Maybe the document on the thumb drive will tell us more." Martin had guesses but nothing solid. Also, they were far away from his parents' house, where the thumb drive waited for them. Paige frowned, like she was thinking the same thing.

She tilted her head a little and asked, "If you were those men chasing us, casing this area, trying to find us, what would you do?"

He had been asking himself the same question. "The place is large and difficult to contain, so first I'd try to find a way to get a smaller area to work with. Which means I'd look at the escape routes and try to block them off."

He nodded toward the road. "I'm guessing these houses

are a mix of permanent residents and weekenders, so on a rainy weekday, some of them will be empty. Your cabin isn't far, and since you're on foot, I'd assume there's a good chance you know someone in the area. You'd go there and ask for help, so I'd be checking the cabins."

She followed his line of thinking. "Makes sense. How would you approach it?"

"Ideally with a map."

"It sounded like those men had looked at one when they referred to this place," she said.

"Or they know the area," he added. "Tell me about the layout of this neighborhood."

She gestured downhill. "The road goes toward the lake, then makes a big loop around it."

"That's great for them." Martin nodded. "If they're in a hurry, they can split up and make their way around the lake in opposite directions. One waits at the place where the road splits, and the others work their way around."

"So you're guessing that these men knock on doors, pretending they lost their cat or something?"

"In my line of work, I'd say who I was looking for, show a photo and assess their reaction," he said. "Meanwhile, someone watches windows from different angles to see how the rest of the house reacts to a knock on the door."

She frowned, and he could see the fear in her eyes.

"This isn't the first time she's been on the run," he added softly. "She probably knows how to lie low when someone's on her tail."

"So they look at all the places first, with the lights on, and then if they don't find them, they start with the other places."

Martin squinted through the fog, trying to count the lights. "How many houses total in this area?"

"Not many. Maybe twenty?"

"Hopefully enough to occupy them for a bit."

She nodded. "Let's go."

"Wait." He took a deep breath. "When we get to your friend's place, we'll need to wait and observe it for a bit before we approach."

Her brow furrowed.

"If you feel like you're close, you might want to run straight for her," he said carefully. "But that's not in her best interest. If she's being watched, then we're all caught. And if she's already caught, we need a different plan."

"I see," she said quietly, but he could feel the thrum of excitement building in her, the idea of finding her sister. He knew how badly she wanted to see Layla.

"And remember, she might not be here." He said it so gently, so softly, trying to silently tell her he understood she was banking all hopes on this one solution. Just like in the cave. He knew how close she was to collapse and that she didn't know what she would do if her sister wasn't here, how she would make it. He remembered how close the twins were growing up and their bond had always fascinated him, and in adulthood, their connection was still as strong. Paige wouldn't rest until she'd found Layla.

She swallowed. Nodded. "I understand."

"We will do everything we can to find her," he said, keeping his voice both warm and firm. He just hoped that was enough.

Martin moved to get up, but Paige placed a hand on his arm. "Wait. I just saw movement."

"Where?" Martin kept his voice low, barely a whisper.

Paige pointed across the main road, a few yards up into the forest. "Just above that boulder."

He watched for a while but didn't see anything. And then…yes, there it was. More of a shadow than a figure, but it was there.

"I guess this suggests we were right about where those men from the mine were headed. Someone is here, and they don't want to be seen."

He scanned their surroundings. The slope of the hill had blocked the view when they'd come around the curve, but here, farther uphill, they'd be directly in sight if they stepped away from the log pile. "We'll need to go back the way we came, then cut through the forest."

Paige glanced behind them, into the dark woods, and nodded. Slowly, they moved backward, using the steepness of the slope to their advantage. Farther downhill, they turned, heading for the subdivision. Lights blinked and grew brighter through the misty trees, revealing a yard at the bottom of the road. They followed a mountain stream downhill, probably the feeder for the lake. He could make out six houses with lights, which would hopefully be the ones the men tried first.

The mountainside flattened into a valley, tucked away in a crevasse between two peaks. Paige led the way, keeping to the forest, beyond the carefully landscaped yards cleared of trees for fire protection. As they crept by, he could make out a couple sitting on two ends of a sofa, watching television inside one of the homes.

A flash of movement caught his eyes, and he froze. They were far downhill from where they'd seen the first figure. Had they just found more of Layla's pursuers?

"Someone else is out here," he said, gesturing between

the house they were passing and the next one. He and Paige watched motionlessly until it happened again.

She gave a quiet gasp. "It's them."

"We don't know for sure, but we need to assume that."

Martin gestured to bushes just before the road that encircled the lake properties. Paige nodded, and he ran from the forest and crouched behind it. Martin was eyelevel with the hedge. The land seemed to be divided into wedges, giving everyone waterfront lots. The uneven downhill slope meant some properties were easier to see from the road than others. He watched as two people approached a house, making their way around the dark property. The men moved slowly, methodically, checking windows for signs of life.

Martin turned to Paige. "Where's your friend's place?"

"Five houses that way." She pointed down the meandering street. "In the direction they're headed."

He could hear the fear in her voice. Five houses. Not nearly enough. "Can you spot the van those people tried to pull you into yesterday?"

She squinted in one direction, then the other. "I don't see it."

"We need to get to your friend's house soon, before they get close," he muttered. Rushing was exactly what he'd been hoping not to do. That was when mistakes were made. But if they didn't outpace these men, they could get to Layla before Martin and Paige had a chance to warn her.

They moved back into the forest and continued, parallel to the road.

"Here," she said, pointing to a dark lot. From the forest, he could barely make out the silhouette of the house. From what he could see, it was a moderately sized two-story rectangle. Viewed from the front, it looked like one story, but from the side he could see the second story built into the side of the slope. It wasn't much to look at from the front, but he imagined the views of the lake were great.

He glanced down the street for movement, but he saw nothing. They'd have to sprint across the road, then hide somewhere while he checked out the property. But before he could zero in on a place to hide, Paige started forward, out of the forest.

Paige had heard perfectly clear what Martin had said earlier: *If you feel like you're close, you might want to run straight for her.* At the time, she knew it would be hard to resist, but that knowledge was abstract. This feeling was visceral. The men were slowly making their way toward Justine's place, and every cell in her body called to her, begging her to find Layla. She was so close. Paige could feel that her sister was there, inside this house, in the same way she could feel that her sister was in distress.

Back in the mine, she had done her best to push her fears down deeper in order to get Martin and her out of there, but right now, they all flooded back. She needed to see her twin, needed to touch her to know with the same visceral certainty that Layla was safe.

Before she could even register what she was doing, Paige was moving forward. Martin's hand on her arm made her jump. When she turned to him, sympathy was written all over his face, and she was sure he could see the desperation in her expression.

"Just give me a couple of minutes to check it out," he whispered. "That's all I ask."

"The men are so close," she pleaded. "We have to hurry."

"We will." His voice was gentle but strong, and she could feel the calming effect it had on her.

She was shaking, she realized, but she nodded. "Clearly I'm not cut out for the private investigator business."

Martin shook his head. "That's not true. Many PIs work with partners because we're all human. No one can think about everything."

A distant look crossed his face, as if his words were triggering his own fears, too. He blinked, and it was gone.

"Let's cross and head for that shed." He pointed to the far side of the property. "It's backed up against that rise."

They sprinted across the wet pavement to the shed near the front entryway of Justine's place. Panting, she watched the street for movement. Nothing.

"You think they have an alarm?"

"Probably. But I know she's there," she whispered. "I can feel it."

She couldn't explain it any better than that. Martin nodded. "Then let's give it a try."

They approached the front door, and Paige knocked softly. Nothing. She opened the flap to the combination lockbox next to the door, but the key box was missing. She glanced out toward the road. Trees shaded the property from the glare of the streetlight, but they couldn't wait around for too long. Paige knocked again, then went to the window next to the door and tapped on it.

"Layla?" she hissed. "It's me."

Martin followed her as she crept through the flower bed, peering into the window. The excitement she had felt just moments before was fading fast. If Layla wasn't here, where would they look next? As fear built in her chest, the quiet snick of a lock cut through the sound of the rain. She turned and rushed to the door, Martin ahead of her. He turned the handle, and it swung open into the darkness. They slipped in. The air inside was cold and dank, like the place hadn't been used in a while. In front of her was the kitchen and dining room, and the lake glittered through a wide window.

"Layla?" she called, softly. "Are you here?"

"Paige? I thought it was you but… You're here." Her sister's voice was a whisper that found its way to her. Paige's heart jumped in her chest as relief flooded through her. Layla. She had found her sister.

Paige rounded the corner and found Layla crouched by the front window. Her sister's short hair was tucked into a cap, and she was wearing jeans and an oversize sweatshirt. Layla ran to her and threw her arms around Paige. Paige let out a shaky breath as she inhaled the jasmine scent of her sister's shampoo.

"Thank you, God," she whispered as relief poured through her.

"A black van passed by twice." Her sister's voice was shaking.

Paige shuddered. The black van. It was almost certainly the same men who'd tried to abduct her.

"I can't believe you're here," added Layla, and there was a mix of awe and relief in her voice that took Paige's breath away. Her sister had thought she'd have to save herself on her own.

"I'll always find you," Paige said, squeezing her sister tighter before she let go. "I know how you think better than anyone."

"Thank you," she whispered. "Thank you for coming."

Her sister released her, then turned to Martin and threw her arms around him. And for one terrible moment, Paige felt a twinge in her stomach. Was she…jealous? Paige looked away, uneasy. Layla had always been the brighter star, more outgoing, more adventurous, and Paige had always been happy to retreat from any spotlight. But something had shifted with Martin and she was conscious of how much she wanted her bond with him to be special. Different. She pushed that feeling away, the discomfort in this rush of feelings. The whole situation was just overwhelming, she thought to herself. That's why her emotions were messy and at the surface. She was grateful to Martin but they couldn't be more than friends. He'd apologized for ghosting her, and she'd forgiven him, but she hadn't forgotten how that had felt. What if she opened herself to seeing where a different kind of relationship would go, and after a few more dinners, he decided he wasn't interested? It would hurt even worse.

"They're coming this way," said Martin. "Was your plan to hunker down here until they pass?"

Layla nodded. "I think it's our best option."

Paige parked herself on the cold stone floor with her back against the door, out of sight of the windows. Layla and Martin crouched on both sides. They waited. Waited. The cold seeped through her wet jeans, and she started to shiver. A beam of light flashed across the living room, sending her heart racing. The men were just outside. Boots trampled on the porch, and the low murmur of voices seeped under the door. They huddled together, their shoulders touching, and somehow this little detail gave her strength. She reached for Layla with one hand and Martin with the other and closed her eyes, trying to calm herself. They were all together. *Thank you, Lord.*

Above their heads, the handle turned. Paige swallowed

back a gasp. The door rattled against the lock…and then stopped. More low voices, and then they were gone. Layla lay her head on Paige's wet coat and let out a long sigh. Paige's shivers came back with a vengeance. "Do you think we're okay to move around?" she whispered.

"Maybe." Martin gave her a wary look as she shivered next to him. "Just make sure to stay out of sight from the windows."

"You both need to change," added Layla.

"I need to eat," Paige said, unlacing her mud-caked boots.

Layla gestured to them. "What happened?"

"There was a mudslide, right around where the old mine shaft is."

Her sister's eyes widened. "You were there? Paige, don't go near that place. If they know you know about it, they'll go after you, too."

"They're already after me," she said, tugging off her boots. "That's why we're here."

Her sister closed her eyes, shaking her head, like she was just now understanding the position they were in.

Paige set her boots on the rug and rose to standing. "What's happening, Layla?"

"It's a fraud scheme," she said, getting to her feet. "It's complicated, but it involves the discovery of rare earth metals for the electric car and solar battery industry. I was doing a piece on the next wave of mining in California and found a company that claims its metals have been found in formerly abandoned mines in the Sierra Nevada foothills, and they're selling shares. I followed the money trail, but when I contacted the people who seemed to be at the center, I noticed I was being followed. Which made me even more suspicious. I got cornered in Clover Valley a few weeks ago on Main Street."

"They tried with me yesterday, outside the bank," said Paige.

Layla's eyes widened. "What happened?"

"I found the key at the cabin and got the thumb drive from the safety deposit box, but when I was walking out, two men tried to pull me into a black van."

Layla reached for Paige and hugged her. "I'm so sorry."

"I'm okay," she said. "What's on the thumb drive? We tried to look at it but..."

Martin stood up. "But my parents' computer is hopelessly outdated."

"Tell me more about what's going on," Paige said.

Layla sighed. "When they cornered me, I did a lot of digging into properties that had switched hands recently. All the records are on that thumb drive, but I found one in particular next to our property, so I've been looking around. And sure enough, someone had been in there. I suspected they're either mining illegally or running some kind of fraudulent scheme around it, where they're taking speculative money based on false claims about finding something in these mines, something that isn't there. Then, when I got back to the cabin, my laptop was gone, and a truck had blocked mine from getting out. That was when I ran."

Paige listened silently, taking in everything her sister was saying. "Who is it?"

"I've narrowed it down to two powerful families in the area, but technically the buyer is a shell company." Layla shook her head. "They contacted me for a meeting, which I took as a tacit threat, and it escalated from there."

"What do they want?" Martin asked.

"I had a friend help me encrypt the files, and apparently it worked because the men still want to know what I know and they can't access my files without me," she said. "I need to get my laptop back, and they'll probably want to kill or at least delay the story until some deals close."

Paige opened her mouth to ask more questions, but Martin rested a hand on her arm. "Let's talk about that later. Right now, we need a plan for getting out of here." He turned to Layla. "Any chance your friend has a car to loan us?"

Layla shook her head. "I wouldn't be here if she did. There's a snowmobile, but that won't do us much good right now."

"We can try the police," Paige suggested.

Layla shook her head. "No service here, and the storm must have taken out the internet because I'm getting nothing."

Martin pulled out his phone and checked. Frowned. "So we need to leave on foot."

This was how it had always been. Paige's skill was the ability to tune everything else out and attend to the person who was suffering, but Layla and Martin had known how to get them out of any situation. They had worked together. There was that similarity between them, and again, that uncomfortable flash of jealousy tugged at her stomach. People always assumed that twins would be in competition, but it had so rarely been that way with Paige and Layla. They were two very different people with two different paths. So why was this happening right now? Why would she be jealous of a hug or the fact that Layla and Martin worked well together, especially in this situation? Paige pushed that feeling away once again.

"The men seem to be making their way down the street,"

Paige said. "I'm not sure whether it's better for us to leave now, or try to stay the night. I'm thinking stay, mostly because I don't know where else to go. But if you have other ideas..."

"We need to be ready to cover a lot of distance," said Martin, frowning. "We're more than ten miles away from town, and that's assuming we take the road. My car by your cabin is uphill and miles away. It's going to take time and energy for us to get there, and it's getting dark."

They were silent, picking through these less-than-ideal options.

"We're also running on empty," he added.

Paige's stomach growled, making its demands known. "Martin brought dog treats, but we weren't that desperate. Yet."

That comment brought the hint of a smile from Layla's face. "Justine has some food here. And most of the kitchen is out of sight of the windows. I've checked."

Paige glanced into the living room and out the window into the darkness, searching for movement. Nothing. She knew they were far from safe, but she couldn't stop the relief that was coursing through her. If they could just stay out of sight, they'd figure out how to get to safety.

With one last glace at the window, she followed her sister and Martin, heading for the kitchen. Layla handed her a glass of water, and she gulped it down, almost choking. She filled the glass again and caught sight of the dirt that still streaked her hands. The day flashed through her mind—the attack outside her cabin, fleeing on the mountain, the mine, the bats, the mudslide... It was overwhelming and almost unbelievable, such a jolt out of her quiet life. Where was the teenage part of herself who had consoled weeping parents who were stuck on the mountain, helpless, with their injured child?

Paige turned on the water to wash away the dirt and found that her hands were shaking.

Badly. As she pressed on the soap pump, her sister slipped her arm around Paige's shoulders.

"You okay?" Layla asked softly.

She took a steadying breath. "I'm going to make sure I am."

"I'm so, so sorry you got dragged into this."

Paige shook her head. "I don't want you to go through this alone. We'll figure this out."

"Agreed." Martin was standing in front of an open cupboard with a handful of granola bars. He set them on the counter, then took out a jar of peanuts, a package of raisins, a box of energy bars and two bottles of water. Paige's eyes widened, and Martin passed her the peanuts.

"They have your favorite," he said.

"You remember that?"

His eyes softened. "Of course I do."

And for one moment, everything else felt better. She could get through this.

Layla cleared her throat, looking from Paige to Martin. "I'm going to check the windows again, and then we can decide on our path."

Paige's face flushed, and she shoved a handful of nuts into her mouth, quickly focusing on her hunger. Now she couldn't get enough of the small nuts. She knew how quickly her energy could leave her.

Her bare feet were cold against the floor, and her jeans were splattered with mud. As she threw yet another handful of peanuts into her mouth, she shivered. Would Justine have a pair of sweatpants she could borrow and maybe some clean socks?

"I'm going to look for dry clothes for us," she said in a low voice, then headed for the back, toward Justine's old bedroom. She slipped through the door, into the dark room, and hurried across the wooden floor. She stopped in front of the dresser, and as she rested her hand on the knob of the top drawer, she glanced out the window.

Her breath caught in her throat. There was someone just beyond the bush, only a few yards away. And she was almost sure he was looking right at her.

NINE

"Someone saw me. I'm almost sure they did."

Martin froze, the energy bar halfway to his mouth as Paige's frantic whisper traveled down the hallway. *Almost sure.* They had to treat it as if it were true. If he were casing this area and suspected he'd seen movement in this house, he'd head straight here.

Paige rushed into the kitchen, and he could see the devastation on her face in the darkness.

"How many?" he asked.

"Just one."

"Good. That gives us a few minutes before the rest get here."

"I should have been more careful," she whispered again, deep self-recrimination in her words. They had to hurry, but first he needed to comfort Paige. He told himself that they'd have a better chance if she was focused, and that was true, but deep down he knew that wasn't the only reason. Not even the primary reason. A part of him needed to be there for her. Which was exactly what he didn't want.

Still, Martin stood up and put his hands gently on her shoulders. He met her gaze, and her eyes were wild with fear. "It's done, Paige, and we're going to figure this out. We just go with the second plan, to leave."

If they stayed, they would be trapped.

He could see Paige was trying to get herself under control, but the fear was taking over.

"Let's get out of here," Layla hissed from the doorway.

Martin glanced at her, then focused on Paige. He reached deep down, beyond the urgency, beyond the fear that something was going to happen to one of them. *Please don't let that happen, God.*

"There are always things we wish we could change," he said, pouring his regret at letting her go into his words. "It's what happens after these things that makes all the difference, okay? I want you to trust me on that right now. I want you to believe that *now* is what makes the difference."

Paige blinked, and he could see she was taking in his words. She was shaking, probably both from cold and fear, and it triggered that deep protective instinct for her once again. The danger they had been in hit him again, this time harder than in the mine.

He had told himself back on the mountain that he could ignore the feelings for Paige that kept popping up, but the moment he saw Layla, hugged her, he knew it was a lie. Because as happy and relieved as he was that they had found Layla, it wasn't the same. Not anywhere near the same. He felt so different with Paige. And this revelation was followed by another—the revelation that maybe he had known it had always been different with her. In any other situation, he would have retreated until he had an answer, a solution to this mess of feelings brewing inside, but right now she needed help. And that was more important.

"We can do this together," he insisted.

She closed her eyes and took a deep breath. When she opened them, he could see the moment that she decided to believe this, to really trust what he was saying. She straightened up. He brushed his hand over her cheek, and her breath hitched. There were so many things he wanted to say, but he turned away, took his own steadying breath and focused on the present.

"We head for the woods, then uphill to the road," he said, grabbing his boots. "Once we're in the woods, we have a better chance of losing them."

"If we need to split up, we meet at your truck," said Paige, then turned to Layla. "It's on the side of the road, just beyond our cabin."

Her sister nodded.

The problem was that it was all uphill from here. How they would make it back up the incline while eluding their pursuers, well… He would leave that to God. They said nothing, just grabbed their socks and boots.

"Are we ready?" asked Paige.

Martin looked out the front window. The night was still and dark. No signs of movement, but it was impossible to tell for sure. "As ready as we're ever going to be."

"Let's go," said Paige, and she slipped out the door and into the night.

Layla sprinted out, followed by Martin at the rear, keeping an eye on everything. The rain had mostly let up, but clouds still hovered low in the darkness. Drops of rain glistened in the mist, and the patter of rain fell unevenly from trees every time a gust of wind blew through the forest. Then he heard the sound of an engine. His heart jumped.

"We have to run," he said.

He pulled up the hood of his dark jacket and sprinted across the driveway, but it was too late. The van's headlights flashed as it roared down the street. He dashed across the road, but even before they reached the side that circled the lake, he knew he didn't stand a chance. They'd been caught.

* * *

Paige could feel the panic welling up in her again, the same panic she had felt in those moments when she was trapped in the mine shaft. The helplessness. The feeling that she had failed her sister. But now it wasn't just her sister. She had put Martin in danger.

"Stay where you are and don't move," called a man. It was impossible to tell them apart in their all-black clothing and face masks, but this one was taller than the rest with a deeper voice. "Slowly."

Out of the corner of her eye, she saw Layla lifting her hands as she said, "We have no weapons."

"I'll check that for myself." Then he touched his ear, like he had some sort of intercom system and spoke again. "There are three of them. The one we're after, the sister and a man, up on the road."

"I'm going to make a chance for you to run," whispered Layla.

Paige shook her head. "I'm not leaving you."

The fear was radiating through her, each heartbeat pounding in her ears. And then, Martin's words came back to her. *I want you to believe that* now *is what makes the difference.* There was nothing they could do to change what had already happened. Right now, they were in danger, and any wrong move could make this situation horribly worse, so she calmed her mind, searching for something she could do to make this better, to make this somehow easier. And when it occurred to her, she knew it was the right way forward. It was the only way, given the circumstances. "I'm Layla," said Paige. "I'm the one you're looking for. You can let the others go."

Both Layla and Martin stared at her with horror.

"Paige, no," said Layla as Martin cried out, "What are you doing?"

Their voices were tinged with panic, and it hurt, physically hurt to know that she was hurting them. And yet, this was truly the best way forward. She knew so little and therefore could give nothing away. Getting the wrong twin would buy them time. The idea of being trapped in that van was filling her with a kind of terror that she was trying very hard not to think about, but it was the only way out of this.

So she turned to her sister and said, "It's okay, Paige. I'm the one they want."

Layla looked at her, incredulous. She shook her head vehemently. "I am not letting you do this."

Her sister's voice had that final edge to it, so strong that Paige knew her sister wasn't budging. And she wasn't, either.

She met Layla's gaze and felt a calm flood through her. "Then I guess we're doing this together."

The man with a gun was watching them, looking from one to the other.

Martin was scowling. "Or…none of us could go," he muttered.

"Enough," the armed man said.

Paige shivered, partly from the cold, partly out of that sinking feeling that they were stuck. Really stuck. The beams from the headlights shone directly in their eyes, blinding her. Another man jumped out, this one bulkier than the first, and her gaze was drawn to his muddy boots. Probably one of the guys who had followed them into the mine.

"Isn't that the other one?" said one. "How are we supposed to know which is which?"

"That's the one from the mountain," said the other, pointing at Paige. "Look at her boots."

"Take them both," the first man instructed.

"No," murmured Martin.

The man with the gun scowled. "Check them for weapons."

The bulkier man came over, patting them all down, and not gently. He pulled out Martin's cell phone and stuck it in his pocket, then finished his search. In that moment, she could understand why Martin's father had insisted on no guns. Because right now was the moment when they decided whether Martin knew too much to keep alive.

"We're not trying to harm anyone. He hasn't seen you, and he has no car or weapon," Paige said. "He's not involved. He just wanted to help me find my sister. Let him go and we'll come with you."

"You're not in a position to negotiate," said the first man sullenly, pointing the gun.

And then it was quiet. She prayed that they were considering the options. Would they decide that it was better not to take him along? It was either that or they would shoot him right here.

"If you shoot any of us, there's no going back from that," she added.

"It wasn't supposed to be like this," said the bulkier guy over his shoulder. "No casualties. The boss just wants to talk to her."

"Fine," said one man. He gestured to the twins. "You two come willingly, and we'll let this guy go."

She glanced over at Martin and she could see the pain and fear in his eyes.

He hated this solution, but she could also see the understanding cross his face. He would have to swallow his feelings, just like she had, and go with the practical plan. If Martin could get out safely, he could go for help, like they'd talked about before reaching Lakewood Estates. Martin looked from Paige to Layla, then gave an almost imperceptible nod.

"I'm so sorry," she whispered and started for the van. Her heart pumped in her chest as she walked toward the doors. Every single fear from the last two days came back, the panic of being trapped, the big hand over her mouth so she could barely breathe and the feeling that her sister was alone and afraid. And now they were leaving Martin behind.

TEN

The man didn't lower his gun. He watched Martin, his eyes barely visible behind the mask. Thank God for the boss's no casualties order, because Paige and Layla were already in the van. It was too late to set another path. But the man was looking at him like he was assessing what to do in lieu of shooting him.

Martin stood with his hands visible, his eyes moving from the gun to the man's face, searching for some thread of humanity between them. "You can disappear," he said softly. "If I had access to a car to follow you, we would have already driven away."

Martin could barely breathe as the man took in his words, hopefully weighing them. *Lord, I am in your hands.*

"Let's go," called someone from the van.

The man looked at Martin for one more tortuously long moment, then gestured with the gun toward the forest.

"Walk away," he said softly. "And don't let me see you again."

Against every one of Martin's instincts, he turned and walked away from Paige and Layla. The van doors closed with a heavy thump, sending a shudder of dread through him. As the engine revved and sped away, he came to a stop. He turned and watched the red lights travel around the winding road. Both Paige and Layla were inside the van that was driving off into the darkness.

Where were they going? Somewhere in the Tahoe area, maybe even close to Clover Valley, if Layla was correct. He wouldn't be able to narrow the destination down without Layla or the thumb drive…which was miles away. He had to find the twins. All his training had been leading up to this moment, when the stakes were suddenly personal. But he could never have prepared for something like this. No amount of preparation would have been enough.

And so, as he stood there on the empty street, the heaviness of what had just happened settling into his chest and weighing down his body, he found himself closing his eyes, praying. *Lord, let the pain of my most difficult years lead to something good in the world.* He prayed that he could find his stamina, use his experience to find a way to do what seemed impossible. He prayed this would have a good end, the end that Layla and Paige and every single family deserved.

"Let Your light shine through," he whispered.

His prayers floated into the night, disappearing into the sounds of the trees, and somehow, the knowledge that he had spoken those words, gave him a calm in the storm. Then he opened his eyes, watching the taillights flicker. They came to a stop up the mountain, idling there next to the road, and then turned…to the right?

A glimmer of hope ran through him as the mistake registered. The van had turned toward town, which meant they were headed for the mudslide blocking the road. He had just gained some time. The van would be forced to turn around and come back this way, giving him a chance to do…something. This was the break he needed. He just had to figure out what to do about it.

With new energy, he jogged along the pavement, up the hill, running through scenarios in his mind. He could try to block their way but…what was big enough to stop a van?

He hiked up to the top of the hill. On one side, the gleaming entranceway sign peacefully announced the subdivision, as if to suggest that if you lived in a place like this, nothing bad could happen. He looked at the forest, at the pile of logs he and Paige had hid behind…

They would be heavy to lift, and he didn't have much time, but maybe he could build a blockade? That way, he could stop the van when it came back in this direction. They'd be trapped. He ran over to the pile and took a loose log from the side, dragging it until he got to the road. He pulled it across the far lane and left it there, like a barrier, then ran back and got a second one. It was heavy, waterlogged, but he tugged it across the manicured lawn and onto the road. He lay this one on the other half of the road, so that it was blocked on both sides. If he could cut off the van in both directions, they'd be stalled, and maybe he'd find a way to break Paige and Layla free.

His mind raced as he worked, looping through the day, processing the overload of fear and something else. That moment in the house when he'd hugged Layla came back to him, triggering a long-buried memory from junior prom.

He, Layla, Paige, Juana and Benji had gone to prom as a group, a sort of Fabulous Five celebration before the twins moved. His father, the amateur chef that he was, had cooked for the whole group of them, and they had dressed up and taken pictures with their matching search and rescue hats. When they got to the dance, they had hung out together and danced with each other, and somehow he and Paige had found themselves paired up for a slower dance. He remembered a moment when she looked at him, with the playfulness gone and something else shining in her eyes. He had looked away, not knowing what to do with it. She and Layla were moving just two weeks later, so he'd tried hard not to imagine what could have been between them if she would have stayed. He'd tried to forget about it.

The intensity of the last twenty-four hours had dug up that memory that had sat there in his brain, dormant, and the feelings it churned up were still very much alive. They seemed to fall into place. Maybe there had always been something more to their bond. Had she felt the same way that night, or had she simply seen an emotion in him that he wasn't then able to recognize?

Whatever the answer, he had been ready for it today apparently. He cared about Paige, not just as a friend. And now was just about the worst time for that realization to happen. Because the last thing Paige was thinking about was questioning whether their friendship might be something more. She was focused on her sister, and he needed to put his feelings aside and focus on helping them both. If he couldn't do that, he was more of a liability right now.

Martin could do this. He *would* do this. For Paige and Layla. This was his work. He dragged a few more logs onto the road, enough to stop a vehicle. He waited. And waited. But the van didn't come.

Maybe he should have waited in case the vehicle returned, but his legs wouldn't let him wait. His own words came back to him from the house. This was the point where mistakes were made. But this was Paige and Layla, and somehow the logic wasn't helping. He needed to do something. And so he started down the dark road, where the van had disappeared.

"I promise I'll find you both," he whispered into the night air as his jog turned to a run.

* * *

Fear coursed through Paige as the van screeched to a halt, then turned. She and Layla had been shoved onto the middle benches of the van, and when it turned, they jolted one way, then the other. She fell onto Layla, then scrambled to find her seat belt. Fear threatened to overtake her as she looked at the closed doors and thought about the man looming behind them in the back row, holding a gun, watching her every move. Two more men sat in front in stony silence.

But she wasn't alone. Her amazing sister was here. Layla, who always kept a level head in difficult situations. And they had Martin. She knew in her heart that this man would do every single thing in his power to save them. The men had said that someone just wanted to talk with Layla, but no one with a gun just wanted to talk. And so, as the van sped onward, she prayed. When she looked over at her sister, Layla's lips were moving like she was praying, too. As the van lurched forward, heading into the darkness, she reached for her sister's hand.

Where were they going? Who were these people? They were built differently, but there was something about their blue eyes and pale skin tone that looked similar. Layla had said she'd narrowed the possible assailants down to two powerful families. Paige wished she had pressed Layla for more details because now was hardly the time to have that conversation. But she had to think about something other than this suffocating feeling of being trapped inside this van, going to a place farther away from town.

"Where's my laptop?" Layla asked.

"You'll get it back. The boss just wants to see your files."

"A journalist who disappears when she's writing a piece about something your boss is involved in isn't a good look," her sister said as they careened toward the road. "My sister reported me missing, so they're looking."

One of the men snorted. "Sure. We'll see where that goes."

Paige swallowed, remembering the way Mike seemed to push her concerns aside. The police were on the lookout for the van, but what were the chances they'd cross paths with a squad car?

The car was silent. Her sister's voice was so calm, so practiced, and Paige had to wonder how this could be the same person whose voice had shook when she hugged her back in Justine's place. Was it just her instinct to be calm in a crisis, or did she also have practice with this kind of danger?

The last time Layla had gone into hiding was the prison scandal. She had stayed in the cabin for over a month, coming out to make calls and write up her pieces, one by one, and turn them in. Even after the news came out, she had stayed there, knowing that repercussions for the recordings which also involved the wardens and drug trafficking was a real possibility. It wasn't until the article triggered an actual police investigation that Layla had stepped out into the open again. All through that, Layla had been safe at the cabin. She hadn't worried about Paige's safety because she could also disappear into the mountains. Now, nowhere was safe.

"If your boss just wants to talk, why are you taking us against our will?" her sister tried.

The man pulled to a stop. "You agreed to come."

Because of Martin.

"I've written articles that will survive me. Even if you harm me, it will still come out," Layla pressed.

The men in the front looked at each other. They definitely looked alike, especially the blue eyes and dark brows. Were they related? The man in the front passenger side looked from Paige to Layla, then back to Paige. He had an expression on his face, like he was putting everything together now.

"You were the one we grabbed yesterday," he said to Paige, then looked at Layla.

"You're definitely the journalist."

"And she knows nothing," said Layla, and now her voice had hints of fear. "You should know I would never tell my sister what is going on. It makes her susceptible to exactly this kind of danger."

"Enough," the man muttered.

The van was idling at the road, and another man ran down from the hillside, then jumped in the back seat. They started forward, turning right onto the main road…in the direction of where the mudslide had blocked access to town. Paige's heart soared in her chest with a moment of hope. Wherever these men thought they were going, they wouldn't get far. They would need to stop. Which meant there would be a chance to escape.

The men in back were muttering complaints, and the two in front debated where to find cell service. Layla squeezed Paige's hand, and whispered in a low voice, "If you get a chance to escape, you need to take it. They'll let you go like they did with Martin."

"No," Paige snapped under her breath. She wouldn't let her sister do this alone. But when she turned to Layla, her sister's eyes were pleading.

"You're our best hope," whispered Layla. "If you escape, we all have a better chance to get help."

Paige met her sister's gaze, and her heart dropped in her chest. Somehow, she knew exactly what Layla was going to do whenever she had the chance. She was going to create some sort of distraction so Paige would have a chance to escape. Which would mean leaving her sister behind, so soon after she'd just found her. The devastation of it took her breath away. She knew Layla, knew this was how she'd gotten through so many harrowing rescues as teens: by blocking out her emotions and taking the logical path. Once her sister took the first step, Paige had no chance but to follow. Maybe this was all courage really was, just pushing aside fears and moving forward with what she knew was right.

Paige braced herself as the van sped down the slick black asphalt, into the dark night. Patches of fog hung low, and the driver was taking the curves too quickly. If they got to the mudslide and somehow Layla created a distraction, she could run away and hide, then loop back and climb the mountain, find Martin's SUV and…wait for him to show up? While Layla was still captured? This sounded like a terrible plan.

Please, Lord, find a way to keep all of us safe.

The van swerved around one corner as a blur of trees flew by. They passed the path where she and Martin had come down, and she thought back to those moments, how much had happened since then, how far they still were from safety. But she pushed that thought aside and focused.

"Right now, we don't know who you are," Layla said. "You let us go and it's only the boss that this can be traced to, not you."

"And that's how we intend to keep it," the driver snapped.

Paige remembered her sister's negotiation tactics, to keep people talking, to stretch out these conversations, digging for information, putting together a bigger picture. She supposed that worked just as well for a journalist as it did for negotiating with kidnappers.

"What happens after I talk to the boss?" her twin asked.

"Talk to him about it," the man in the passenger's seat muttered.

Paige tuned out that conversation as she focused on another problem. She'd seen the mudslide as a possible diversion, but what if they hit it? The rocks and logs had fallen just beyond a curve in the road, and at this speed under the darkness and fog, the driver wouldn't have time to stop.

"You're going too fast," said Paige. "There's a mudslide just ahead."

The driver met Paige's gaze through the rearview mirror and scowled. "You're telling me how to drive now?"

A new panic bubbled up in her stomach. "Seriously," she insisted. "It's coming up right after this next curve."

She whipped around at the two men behind her. "Tell him."

The two looked at each other, and she could see the uncertainty in their eyes.

"I'm not sure where—"

"It might be—"

"Silence!" the driver yelled as they whipped along the road.

As they rounded the curve, his last words faded as the mudslide suddenly appeared in front of them. The driver slammed on the brakes as the van careened straight toward it. She clung to her seat belt and braced her feet against the seat in front of her.

The driver yelled out an expletive as the breaks screeched. The van hit the mud with a hard thud and lurched to a stop. The airbags exploded, filling the car with a cloud of white dust as the men behind them flew against the back of the twins' seat. One landed face down between them. She turned to Layla, and through the white cloud, she saw fear in her sister's eyes. Her sister was always the brave one, the leader, but right now it was Paige's turn to be brave. Her sister had been running longer than Paige had. She'd been alone in the cabin, and she needed support as much as Paige did. So she looked into her sister's eyes and said, "I'll do this. I promise." And she felt that promise run through her down to her core. In the end, she wasn't particularly brave, but she would do anything for her sister. Which was what this came down to.

Through the haze of airbag dust and tangled limbs, she found the buckle to her seat belt. Snapped it. Found her sister's and did the same. Opened the door. Grabbed Layla's hand. Stumbled out, pulling her sister behind her.

Layla tottered out into the night and fell back against the van door. She couldn't walk. Was she injured or just in shock from the crash? The men's grunts and snaps rang behind her, but she blocked them out. Paige slung her sister's arm around her shoulder and lifted her, channeling all the strength she used in her daily work. They stumbled forward, onto the pavement, listening for signs of pursuit.

A rumble of an argument broke out in the van. Paige and Layla stopped at the concrete ledge of the road.

"I can't walk." Her sister's voice was raw, desperate. "You have to go without me."

Paige stood on her tiptoes, straining for a view of the road, trying to figure out her next move. Then she glanced back at the van. One man stumbled out of the side doors and sat down next to the car. The driver's side door swung open, and the tall man climbed out.

"Go," Layla urged. "Go find a way to help me."

Paige's body refused to move. How could she leave—

"*Please*, Paige. I can't outrun them, but you can. And then you can help me."

The desperation in her sister's voice rattled her, so she overrode every instinct inside, jumped the guard rails and fled.

ELEVEN

Martin almost tripped when he heard the screech of tires and the crunch of metal and glass echoing across the mountain. It was as if his heart jumped into his throat. He gasped for air. That sounded way too much like a car crash, and the only vehicle around was the van.

What had happened to Paige and Layla? Were they hurt?

The heavy thump of the van, the sickening crack of bending steel… No, he couldn't let himself consider it. He needed to find them. Martin sprinted down the road, his body filled with purpose. His stride widened, and he tuned all his senses to the wet pavement, the sound of the trees, the scent of wet asphalt, and searched for sounds from the van that had disappeared behind curve after curve of the mountain road. How far away was he?

He rounded one curve, then another, hugging the side of the road, squinting through the fog. He searched for headlights or taillights, something to tell him that he was on the right path, but only darkness and the incessant rain surrounded him. He willed his legs to move faster, but they burned from strain and overuse. Another curve. Another. As he rounded the next one, he could make out something in the road. Faint voices wafted through the foggy night, deep male voices, and then they disappeared. He ignored his exhaustion and sprinted forward. In the mist, the shape of a van appeared, eerily still.

Everything in his body told him to run to the van, to help, and his exhaustion was making it hard to focus on anything else. But there was too much on the line to make a mistake. Martin stopped by the side of the road, closed his eyes and focused. He slipped across the road and into the forest, just downhill out of sight of the road. He traced the path of the road until he came to the place where the mudslide poured across the road in a mess of dirt, stones and trees, bending the guardrail and spilling farther down the mountain. Martin ran up the embankment and peered over the tangled metal of the guardrail. The van door was open, and a thin white haze floated inside. Smoke? No, he would have smelled it by now. He caught sight of a deflated airbag in the front seat. He listened for noises, but all he could hear was the wind and the drips of rain from the trees and the night insects singing their songs. He crept closer and peered in the open doors, afraid of what he might see. Empty. They had escaped, all of them.

Thank you, Lord. This was a gift, not one to be taken for granted.

Martin took a long steadying breath and studied the area. He moved around the van to the front, to the mud-caked license plates. He picked up a rock and scratched off the dirt so the letters and numbers appeared. This would be easier with his phone, but the men had taken it. He'd have both a flashlight and his camera to document it all. His memory for this kind of thing was usually excellent, but his emotions were wreaking havoc on his focus. He studied the numbers and letters, using his usual memory technique of creating a narrative with them that he'd remember: *9* was the number of years since the Fabulous Five broke up, *M* stood for Main Street, where he'd first seen Paige yesterday… He rehearsed the story in his mind again and then moved on to inspect the rest of the van. He crouched by the door he'd seen Paige and Layla disappear into, ignoring the twist in his gut this memory provoked and focused on the footprints. They were a mess, as if everyone had tumbled out of the car at once. They were hard to follow through the debris, but it looked as if they'd crossed through the mudslide's trail and not single-file.

More footprints. They were there and then stopped, almost like they had waited and then continued. Martin's heart soared as he moved along those footprints. He was onto something. He continued to track, and as he reentered the forest, he found footprints through the ditch, where the mudslide had spilled, but then there was nothing.

He climbed over charred tree trunks and stepped through the wet dirt. Hints of voices floated down the mountains, and he tried to follow them into the dark forest. Now he had to follow his instincts, to think like they would think. He searched the ground for more sets of prints, but the ones he found weren't human. They were large, four pads with claws in front of them. It was a wildcat, the size of…a bobcat maybe? He'd seen a few back when he'd lived in Clover Valley. Bobcats would avoid people if they could, so he pushed that thought away.

Another murmur of voices floated down the mountain. He froze, trying to pinpoint the direction. They weren't as far as he had thought they might be, and that gave him hope. He started up the steep hill, moving faster, trying to stay behind boulders and shrubs. The fog and the night were his covers, and the drive to protect, ingrained in him for as long as he remembered, warred with exhaustion as he picked his way up the incline.

And then, finally, he saw movement. It wasn't much, just a shimmer of white, but it was there. Another grumble of voices. He was gaining on them, and fast. But that thought was followed by another that made his stomach drop. He had been far behind when he heard the crash, so he should be much farther behind them now. The only reason he could think that the group might move this slowly was that someone was injured. That thought sent a shudder of fear through him as he continued up the hill. It would be a challenge to break the twins away from their captors, but if Paige or Layla were injured? That idea was a piercing arrow inside him, and he couldn't ignore it. How would he get them off the mountain?

He moved faster, faster, slipping behind trees. And then he caught sight of three shadows, moving slowly up the hill. In the center was a figure who slowly limped up the hillside, arms around the shoulders of the other two. The center person was shorter, short enough to make him worry. Was it Paige or Layla? A little rumble of words came from one, then the other. He strained to listen, but Martin could only make out a few words.

"Top…truck…boss…motel…"

Motel. Was that where they were headed? To meet someone? It made sense, somewhere they could pay cash, where they wouldn't be seen entering and leaving in the dead of night. No hallways to contend with, no neighbors. There must be a handful of motels in the area, though he could only think of one off the top of his head. Twin Pines Motel right in the center of Truckee—not a good place to stay under the radar. Paige might know of more lodgings.

That thought landed with a sickening thud. He counted the figures in front of him. Three in a row, one ahead, one behind… He could only see five figures total moving slowly up the mountain. Earlier they'd surmised there were four men in total. Was someone missing? Was it one of the twins? It was too hazy to make out the jacket or any other details that might tell him who was out there. Martin continued up the hill, keeping the five figures in sight, trying to make sense of what he was seeing. Someone was missing, and they didn't seem to be looking for that person.

What happened? If it was one of the twins, how would he even begin to find her? And how was he supposed to do that without leaving Layla at the mercy of these men? He was stuck, pulled in all directions, and time was ticking. *Please, Lord, show me the way forward. I can't leave either of them behind.* Martin closed his eyes, and he felt a rush of relief as the prayer flowed through him. It was as if something had opened inside him, and he could talk to God again, like he used to. It was a balm that soothed this ominous feeling of danger and helped him think straight. *They're moving slowly*, he reminded himself.

But the trees made their own noises in the night, branches cracking and shushing in the wind. The mist had settled inside the forest, giving it an eerie glow in the moonlight. Slowly, he circled the party, keeping his distance. And then, out of the corner of his eye, from the opposite direction, he caught a glimpse of movement. Was it a person? Slowly, so slowly, he started toward that shadow of movement that he was almost sure he saw, listening, watching.

Then he saw it again. The animal was small, like an overgrown cat. Martin slowed his pace, wary as it wandered up the hill, sniffing, then changing direction. It was black with rounded ears and a tail swishing through the darkness. The size made it look like a bobcat, but this was no bobcat. It was a panther cub, and its shiny black coat was beautiful. But where there was a small cub, there was almost certainly a mother. He squinted in the fog, searching for an adult, but saw nothing. Still, the air around him felt charged with an energy that put him on alert. Most big cats were reclusive, coming out at night.

The cub continued up the mountain, exploring in the direction of the five people Martin was following. Martin's heart pounded harder. Watching the cub's path, there was a good chance that they could all be between the mother and the cub.

Big cats generally avoided people rather than confronting them, but the one exception was when their cubs were vulnerable. Mothers wouldn't hesitate to protect them. Were they all headed into the middle of this panther's territory? If so, they were walking toward certain danger.

Paige hid just out of sight as she watched her sister painfully limp over the rough terrain of the mudslide, wincing every time she put weight on her right ankle. She could feel the depth of that pain. She couldn't block it out. But she had kept herself hidden, keeping her distance as the group started into the forest and up the mountainside. And then Paige followed them, climbing over the rocks and muddy branches, then darted across the road to start up the mountainside.

She stayed far enough away, just out of sight, listening to the low noises of the party, making their way up the mountain, carrying Layla with them…but what next? They had seen a silver truck parked by the side of the road on the drive in, just before the last curve to her place. Was that where the group was headed? If so, before the group reached that truck, Paige needed to find a way to separate Layla from them because if her sister got into that car, she was gone.

Everything in her screamed to run toward her sister, to close the distance between them and then... What could she do? She had to be smart about this. She had to think through it. Martin's words from the house came back to her, his encouragement to keep her mind on the present. She forced away the terror that threatened to overwhelm her and reached for the calm that she knew was somewhere deep inside her. *Let me find You, Lord. Please, guide me here.* It was the space inside her that she had carved out, the place she held onto deeply, where she could connect with God. Though everything was bleak and terrifying around her, she grabbed hold of that little kernel of hope inside her and hung onto it for dear life.

Keeping that thought close, Paige made her way up the mountain, wracking her brain for ways to break up the group. She had four men to contend with, and at least one had a gun. She was alone.

That thought was interrupted when the hair stood up on the back of her neck. It felt like someone was watching her. Someone or...something? She had no idea what it was, but something was putting her on high alert. Slowly, she turned. Looked around. The night around her was still, and quiet. Ominously. And she felt a shiver run through her. She was not alone.

Had one of the men slipped away, looking for her? Or was it something else?

She was exposed. She had always been comfortable in the forest—it always felt welcoming—but tonight, there was a threatening edge to the darkness. Was it just the attackers, or was there something more?

She searched her surroundings once again. There was movement, but it was so hard to see anything. She jumped at the snap of twigs behind her but saw nothing. The heavy mist had settled after the rain, cloaking the mountainside, forcing her to rely on other senses. The smell of decay radiated from the forest floor as the rain fell, and the sounds of the night were everywhere, wings fluttering, mosquitoes buzzing in her ears. But the noise she'd heard was something else, a soft crunch of wet leaves.

She heard it again. Something had moved, something low to the ground, and she whipped around, then stood still. Another mosquito buzzed in her ear, and she batted it away, trying to focus on the forest. And then she saw what looked like an overgrown black house cat creeping by. A panther cub. It was wandering behind the crowd, as if it was just as interested in the group making its way up the mountain as she was. The thought made her shiver because a cub wouldn't know better. A cub would do things just for fun, unlike its more focused parents. A cub would stalk them just for the sake of curiosity.

The urge to warn Layla was overwhelming, and she clamped her hand to her mouth to force herself not to call out. She stood stock-still, searching for what to do. Then, as she watched, the panther looked her way. She stood up and raised her hands, flapping them wildly over her head. If it came at her, she was going to have to scream, giving away her location. The cub looked in the direction of the group, then back at her, as if it was debating its possibilities. Then Paige caught a glimpse of movement behind the cub, making its way out of the mist. Another cat, much larger. The mother. Her heart jumped in her chest.

She knew running was the most dangerous thing she could do. It would turn this into a game for this cub to play. But it was so hard to stay in place and face these cats, knowing that even just a playful curiosity would likely be the end of her. Paige's breaths came in pants, and she was trying to hold them in, trying not to give away her spot, but it was just too much. Then, the cub seemed to decide. It took one last look in the direction where Layla was disappearing, and then turned to her. Took a step, then another step, as if testing this new idea. The mother stayed behind, watching her cub, and Paige had no doubt that the mother was ready to pounce whenever the cub needed her. She made eye contact, frantically waved her hands over her head, the way she had been taught during ski patrol training, trying to make herself appear bigger, but the cat just stared at her, undeterred. Paige was so far outmatched. Her time to act was running out. She had tried two tactics, and neither were working. She couldn't wait any longer, so she made the choice between the two dangers. She screamed.

The cub in front of her startled, stopping in its tracks, so she did it again, letting out all her fears from the day. She screamed out her frustration with how scared she was to be stuck on the mountain, to be vulnerable to people who were doing the wrong thing. All these feelings flooded through her as she screamed and screamed.

And then, there was another scream, one from behind her, she whipped around and saw Martin sprinting toward her, his hands in the air, waving them. Martin? He was here. He had found her. Somehow, in all this mess, he had found her. *Thank you, Lord.* A rush of warmth and resilience ran through her. He was here for her. He had somehow done it. And now he was putting himself in danger for her.

There was noise up the hill, shouts. The men were shouting at each other, but she couldn't afford to listen right now. She turned back to the cat. It had stopped in its tracks, but it wasn't retreating. She screamed again as Martin came up to her. She glanced over at him, and his eyes were filled with alarm. Slowly, he reached in his pocket and threw a spray of something. The dog food? He took out another handful and threw it. It rained down around the cats. The panthers growled…then sniffed. Paige's heart soared as the cat turned to the side and buried his nose in the ground, where one of the treats had landed.

Martin threw another handful, and this time, the mother bowed her head and found a bite. Then he slipped his hand in Paige's and said, "We need to back away. Slowly."

TWELVE

Martin's senses were on high alert. The panthers in front of them were distracted, but he had no idea how long that would last. Then there were the voices of the men, way too close to them.

"They're following us," said one.

"You should have gotten rid of them right away," muttered another.

These men had no idea the cats were there. Martin considered yelling out a warning, partly for Layla's sake but also for the sake of the cats, in case one of the men got the bright idea of shooting at them. But any sound might bring both dangers closer.

He tried to keep his eye on the panther mother and cub as he and Paige backed up. They were still in the same place, as far as he could see, gathering up the dog treats he had thrown in different directions. But the mist was making it hard to see them, which meant he would no longer be able to track their location. The panthers, on the other hand, would have no trouble tracking him. Martin had no idea what the cub would do next. Would he be satisfied with the dog treats and move on, or would he continue to track one of the other groups? The thought made him shudder, but he forced himself to focus on the next steps.

A man muttered a couple expletives, and that was followed by more mutterings.

"Silence." The new voice was like a whip, hard in its certainty, unmistakable in its threat. "You. Go find them."

"Should I shoot them?" came the response.

"I don't care what you do at this point. Just get them off our tail. And if you're not back at the truck by the time we get there, we'll pick you up later."

From the muttering Martin heard in response, he could tell the man wasn't happy about that plan. Next to him, Paige let out a shaky breath.

"Are you hurt?" His voice was barely there, but he knew she had heard it because she swallowed, then shook her head.

"You?"

It was hard to tell right now. His body was like a live wire. "No. What are we going to do about Layla?"

"I… I don't know. But she's hurt. She twisted her ankle, and she wanted me to go." Paige's voice was quivering, and he could hear how wrenching that decision had been, how painful it had been to leave her sister behind. She met his gaze, and her eyes were pleading. "I had no choice. It's her best chance."

It was the same argument they had used with him not so long ago, that he should take his chance to escape because it was their best chance to find help. And he had, in fact, found her again. But right now, he could see that she understood just how much harder that plan was from the other side. He laced his fingers with hers. Maybe it was for her comfort or maybe for his own, but that feeling that had fluttered through him before took off again.

"We'll find a way to get her free." There was determination and so much purpose behind that statement, a purpose that he felt bone-deep inside him. He would help make this right for her. He cared so deeply for her. He'd hated being separated from her when the men took her, wondering what was happening and if she'd come to harm. The relief at finding her in the woods had felt overwhelming. And the realization of just how much he cared about her had him nearly staggering back.

She could hear that purpose in his voice, he was almost sure, because something softened in her gaze. She nodded.

Voices made their way up the hill, grumbles, and shouts from the men.

"We have to go," he said. "Which way?"

She let go of his hand and pointed back toward to mudslide. "It's rockier this way, so there's more chance for cover."

Martin followed her across the mountainside, keeping an eye uphill, looking for the man who had been sent out to find them.

"If they see me again, they'll kill me and make it look like an accident," added Paige.

The words were a punch in his gut. *Please, Lord, continue to keep her safe.* Because they weren't anywhere near safe yet.

"I'm not going to let that happen." His voice sounded calmer than he felt. *God willing.*

"The men are heading for a truck, and I'm almost sure it's the silver one we saw," whispered Paige.

"We need to get to my car. I heard them mention a motel," he said.

"We can do this," she whispered.

The comment gave him a little tiny spark of hope. Because despite everything that had happened—despite the fact that she'd been alone on the mountain, separated from her sister and him—he could hear that she was gathering her strength for whatever they'd face next. They'd made it through so much today. As long as they both kept their focus, there was a chance they could make it out of the forest in time to follow the silver truck and save Layla. Another surge of emotion for her bubbled up in him, strong, powerful, and he didn't want to think about what it meant. Not here, not right now.

They turned, starting up the hill, back toward the mudslide, north of her grandmother's cabin. Paige moved along the slope with an agility that showed how at home she was in the forest. There was a rustle behind him, and he turned around as he moved, but the fog and the forest shrouded everything. They hiked through the darkness, continuing up the mountain. The farther they went, the more he could hear Paige's heavy breathing.

They rounded a large boulder, and she stumbled. Paused. He could see that Paige's energy was waning. She was going slower than she had been earlier in the day, and he probably was, too. The only thing they'd had to eat since breakfast were the handful of snacks, and his own thighs burned from overuse. They were both headed for a crash, and they weren't anywhere near safe.

The rain was finally letting up, just a patter on the trees. His coat had held off the rain well, but nothing else had, and he was trying hard not to think about how wet and tired he was.

A shuffle came from behind the boulder. Had the man found their footprints in the dark, or had they caught the cub's interest again? Martin hiked on, praying the man was just as exhausted as he was, praying that the panthers had moved on.

They were out in the open again, making their way

through the fog, when he caught movement out of the corner of his eye. He whipped around, and a figure stepped out of the darkness.

"Put your hands where I can see them," said a voice as a man stepped out of the mist. He was pointing a gun directly at them.

Everything inside Paige wanted to give up. She wanted to fall onto the ground and just let the next few minutes take their course. And she might have, if she were alone, if no one was depending on her. But she wasn't alone. Martin's life and Layla's life were at risk, and she couldn't give up on them. She had to do something. But what could she do? There was a man pointing a gun at her, and they were in the middle of a forest.

Paige closed her eyes and prayed. She prayed for her sister's safety and Martin's safety and her own safety, because her own death would leave Layla with the kind of loss that she was so afraid of right now. *Tell me what to do right now, Lord. Tell me how to save us.* Nothing came to her. But she knew that prayer didn't work that way. It wasn't a magical solution for her problems, but, oh, how she wanted it to be right now. She wanted someone to tell her what to do. Still nothing came. But she couldn't wait around for a sign. Especially not now. *I need to help myself. I need to trust God to guide me.*

She focused on everything she had picked up from Layla over the years. It was best to keep the person talking, to find a hook. Her sister had used this tactic earlier in the van. Talking was the only tool Paige had.

"We're no threat to you," she said. "We don't know who you are, and you have my sister. We're just trying to get back to our truck."

All of these words were true, and yet he didn't lower his gun. His eyes were obscured in the darkness, and it was impossible to read him. All she could feel was the tension of this moment vibrating through her.

"Have you thought about what it means to have someone's death on your hands?" asked Martin. "What it would mean to live with that?"

The man swallowed, and the hard set of his jaw softened for a moment before the tension was back. Had Martin found an angle? Her heart soared.

"What does it take for someone to deserve to lose their life?" added Martin quietly. She had to wonder from his tone if he had considered this question, too. She had thought about this question, long and hard, when her father had urged her to get a gun "for her protection" when she was living alone.

But she had turned the question around: would she pull a gun on someone who was threatening her? That question led inextricably to another: would she shoot someone, knowing it was possible to take that person's life? Or even if she shot only to wound, was she willingly causing someone else pain, excruciating, awful pain, that they would possibly never recover from?

Paige had prayed on that question for a long time, but in the end she had known the answer all along. She wasn't willing to do that to another person no matter who that person was. Who was she to make a judgment like that, to be the one to hurt someone? That judgment was for the Lord, not her.

Had Martin worked his way through these considerations, too? As they stood on the other end of this equation, she knew she had made the right decision.

"I don't have to kill you," said the man, and his hard expression didn't falter this time. "There are things I can do to make sure you don't make it off the mountain, the forest will take care of the rest."

Paige shuddered as she flashed back to the two big cats, the baby and the mother panther, watching them.

"We just want to get out of the rain and end this, just like you," said Martin gently. "We don't know you. We have nothing you want."

"You haven't done anything we can prove," said Paige. "It's our word against..."

The sentence died inside her as she caught movement out of the corner of her eye. From behind the rock, she saw the headfirst, then the tail. The panther cub had followed them. Which meant the mother wasn't far behind.

Paige was frozen in place. They were being hunted from both sides. She looked from one threat to the other, trying to decide which attacker was the most dangerous. The wild animal had no malice but no compassion or understanding for her. It probably only saw her as something to explore. The armed man was filled with malice and fear, but somewhere inside him there was compassion. She had seen it for a moment on his face. Could she figure out how to tap back into that?

She saw the moment when the man spotted the animal. His eyes widened, and he took a step back.

"We saw this cub before, and she's caught our scent again," said Martin in a soothing voice, louder this time now, as if he was also trying to warn off the cub.

The man's eyes flashed with fear, but they changed almost immediately with a hard look of determination.

"I'll take care of that," he said, and he swung his gun around and pointed it at the cub.

"Don't shoot it," urged Martin, panic filling his voice as

the man cocked the gun, letting the bullet drop into place, and aimed. "The mother—"

But before Martin could finish his sentence, the gun went off. A deafening boom rang over the hillside, echoing through the fog. The cub yelped and skittered. Paige jumped back, her gaze fixed on the cub, straining to see if it was hit.

Then, she heard a growl. The mother. She was close. Paige whipped around in the darkness, and the mother panther sprang from the forest, lunging at the man from behind. The shooter pitched forward onto the ground, and his gun went off again as it flew from his hand, another deafening boom that shattered in Paige's ears. The cub let out another yelp, darting one way, then the other.

Paige was paralyzed in place for one long moment, and then her rescue instincts kicked in.

"Don't fight it," she called to the man. "Play dead. That's your best chance."

Before she could register what happened next, Martin grabbed her hand and gave it a tug. There was a part of her that thought everyone deserved to be healed, a part that wanted to help this man, but Martin's survival and her own were on the line.

"Cover your head and play dead!" she yelled as she slowly backed away into the mist, praying that the mother and cub wouldn't follow them.

As soon as they were out of sight, Martin squeezed her hand and tipped his chin uphill, and she nodded back. The growls and grunts were painful to listen to, and as she let go of his hand, her heart ached so much that it took her breath away. She was leaving this man in danger, and her sister was somewhere on this mountain, injured and vulnerable. Still, she climbed the hill, following the edge of the mudslide. Her lungs burned and ached, but she pushed on. They had been granted a reprieve, and she was not going to waste it. How many more close calls would they survive? They stomped through streams of runoff and muddy trails until finally, finally, they reached the road.

"This way," she panted, pointing toward the turnoff, where they had left his car.

And then it was there, emerging out of the mist, like some kind of oasis. Martin's SUV was still there. They had found an escape, a way to catch up with Layla. She hadn't let herself hope until right now. She raced to the door and jumped inside, panting. She lay her head back, hearing Martin's breaths next to her, as her heart banged in her chest, hours of exhaustion and fear pounding through her. When her breathing began to slow, she finally looked over at Martin. It was only then that she saw he had been shot.

THIRTEEN

Thank you, Lord.

Martin had prayed more in the last twenty-four hours than he had in years. Sure, he'd said his amens in church along with the rest of the congregation and bowed his head at the right time, but he had felt the distance growing, a coldness where there once was warmth. He hadn't registered just how far he had drifted until right now, when the comfort flooded through him, the way it used to so many years ago. It was a little absurd since his arm felt like it was on fire, but through the pain, something bigger rose in him. He was so grateful that Paige was safe next to him, that they'd found the safety of his SUV, that somehow, against all reasonable expectations, they had made it out of the forest.

What a strange thing this was, to feel thankful in a crisis. But it felt like an awakening, a long time overdue, and he felt lighter. Maybe this is what he needed, so he decided to accept that, however it had come. Faith was a mysterious thing, and he was the last one to explain how it worked.

Paige was staring out the front windshield, her eyes distant, but as her breathing had slowed, she turned to him and gasped.

"You're…you're shot," she whispered. "You're bleeding."

"The bullet must have skimmed my shoulder," he mumbled. There was no way to downplay a bullet wound, but he was going to give it his best.

"We have to get to the hospital," she said, and he could hear the rising panic in her voice.

He nodded. "But we need to find your sister first."

She grimaced, as if the choice she was now facing made her physically sick. "I can't make you wait."

"Yes, you can," he said, trying not to wince at the intense burning that was radiating down his arm. "Just bandage me up, and we'll find the motel where your sister is. We can call the cops and then go to the hospital."

She shook her head. "I'm a nursing assistant and most of my patients are over sixty-five," she said. "Gunshot wounds don't usually come up in my line of work."

"I trust you," he said softly. "Just do your best."

Paige closed her eyes. Swallowed. Let out a deep breath. "Can you get your arm out of your jacket and sweatshirt? We can try to pull up the sleeve of your T-shirt and take a look."

Unzipping his jacket was straightforward. He could do that with his left hand. But taking both the jacket and his sweatshirt off was not nearly as straightforward…and definitely much more painful. He winced as he shifted in his seat, and she winced, too. He was trying so hard to keep the pain off his face, but it was impossible.

"We can't do this. You're in so much pain." Paige's voice quivered.

"It's not going to be easier at the hospital. I still have to take my sweatshirt off."

"They'll cut it off. Actually, if you have a first-aid kit somewhere in here, we should do that."

He nodded. "Sounds infinitely better than moving that arm." He gestured to the trunk and tried not to shiver. The jacket was the only thing keeping him marginally warm right now.

He popped the back hatch, and then turned on the car, setting the heat at full blast. If he wasn't careful, he could go into shock. Paige hopped out of the car and returned a moment later with the first-aid kit. She opened it and pulled out a thick pair of scissors. He closed his eyes and shivered as the cool air hit his arm, sending needles of pain down it. He turned his head away so Paige wouldn't see the way he gritted his teeth every time something moved over the wound. The snip of the scissors filled the quiet car, and he gritted his teeth harder when she pulled the material from his shoulder.

"Sorry," she whispered, adjusting the remaining part of his jacket far from the wound.

He shook his head. "Continue."

"This is going to hurt," she added.

He had to wonder what she meant, considering the fact that it already hurt. "Just do it."

A cold antiseptic wipe touched his wound, sending a new burst of searing pain through him, and then she pressed a large wad of gauze against the gash. As she taped the gauze in place, he opened his eyes again to inspect the wound.

Paige looked up at him, her brown eyes filled with apology. "Thank God the bullet just grazed you. I did the best I can for now, but we need to get help."

"We will. After we locate your sister." He finally looked back at her. She was so caring and beautiful and kind, always looking out for others. He'd appreciated that about her even as teens. He knew he should thank her and move on, shut off these feelings, just for a little longer. Just until they were safe…

"You okay?" she asked.

A tide of emotions rose inside him, and right now, as he looked in her eyes, he could feel that he was in over his head. The only choice was let himself swim in this sea of feelings.

"I'm just thinking of all the ways that that situation on the mountain could've gone so very wrong," he said. "Seeing you in danger was terrifying."

"You must see a lot of terrifying things."

"I do, but…" He struggled to put what was making this different into words. "I care about you. A lot. I always have, but today—"

Her face lit up, and for one beautiful breath they were back in the restaurant where everything had felt so *right*. When all the more difficult parts of his life fell away, and there was just the two of them, together. But then her face shuttered closed, and she looked away. He didn't know what to read in that, what to say to make that look come back. Later. When this was over, he'd figure out what to do with these…feelings.

"We should get going," he said, and his voice came out rough. "You'll need to drive."

"We're almost to the spot where I saw that truck," she said as the car rounded the bend. They strained their eyes through the mist, searching for the silver truck that had sat by the side of the road on their way up. Was it only hours ago and not days? So much had happened, and she was trying not to focus on this strange mix of hope and fear from the moment before, when Martin had looked at her with what had felt like love. Not the friendship kind of love. Something more. But what if it wasn't? What if they were right back in Sacramento, where she'd read the situation wrong, missed something? But maybe she needed to stop thinking about this in terms of risks for rejection. Here, in the midst of all the fear and tragedy, she had felt something worth fighting for. And maybe that was exactly what she should do—fight for it—even if it meant the risk of making a fool of herself. Once this was over, she'd figure out a way to tell him how she felt.

"Just past here and..." Her voice trailed off. Paige was sure this was the place the truck had been parked, but no one was there. It was just a little patch of dirt and gravel, washed away by the rain. No truck. They were too late.

She looked over at Martin, watching him visibly swallow.

"We lost them." Her voice barely came out.

"It's not over, Paige," said Martin, and she could hear a hard determination in his voice, like he had enough hope to carry them both if she needed to lean on him.

Paige drove into the night, clutching the steering wheel, trying to stop her hands from shaking as the fear threatened to bury her. Her whole body was shaking. Her sister had disappeared again, and what would have happened if the man back on the mountain had moved the gun a centimeter more? That centimeter would mean inches for the bullet's trajectory, and that might've meant the bullet could've entered somewhere that she couldn't patch up. Somewhere that would've left Martin bleeding out on the mountainside. And she would have been there with him, helpless.

She tightened her hands on the cold leather of the steering wheel, trying to focus on the road ahead. Her sister was somewhere out there, injured, scared but defiant. How far behind were they?

Paige wanted to speed up, but they had witnessed one mudslide. It probably wasn't the only one. There were burn scars all over the mountain from the fire last year, and any one of them could trigger a mudslide. Which meant she had to take the road slowly, especially in this fog. The only hope was that the men had learned their lesson and were going equally slowly.

"Are you okay, Paige?" Martin's voice was a balm, not taking away these thoughts but soothing them, comforting them, reminding her in the most absolute terms that the gun had not strayed that extra centimeter. That he was there, next to her.

"I'm so scared," she admitted. "I've tried so hard to make myself a calm life, but there were times when I wanted more. When I felt like I was avoiding my fears instead of living. Now it's like I'm getting years of excitement all in one day."

Martin nodded. "It's hard to know why God chooses our paths."

"But we're in His hands," she said. "I have to remind myself of that."

"Amen."

Thank you, God, for bringing us together. The words echoed inside her, ringing through the loneliness she'd felt these past few years in Clover Valley. She hadn't even fully recognized it, until right now, this feeling that had been growing all day, how good it felt to not be on her own, to not try to do everything by herself. To have someone to lean on, someone there by her side. She wanted Martin to stay in her life.

"Let's go through what we know," said Martin, and she focused on his voice, the strength of it. "Layla said there's someone behind this, someone who wants to meet with her, but she's not sure who. And I heard the word *motel* when I was tracking them, so I think we check the local motels for the silver truck we saw."

She frowned. "We should have stopped and written down the license plate when I had a bad feeling about it this morning. Then we'd have something tangible to give the police, someone to look up."

She knew what Martin's answer would be. *Don't look back. You can't change that. Focus on the now so you don't make mistakes in the present.* Or at least she thought she knew what he'd say, but he said something even better.

"I memorized the van's license plate." He repeated it back to her. "And I have an extra phone in the glove compartment for emergencies."

Her heart sped up as a little glimmer of hope burst inside her. "Thank God. When we get in cell range, you can send that to the police."

She was starting to feel better as she fixed her mind on the problem, forcing her to be analytical. Her teamwork skills were rusty, after so many years off the search and rescue team, but they were still there. *And a part of you missed this*, a voice whispered inside her, memories of her old self.

"How many motels do we have around here?" asked Martin. "They'd want ones without a central entrance, some place where there's no surveillance footage. And they'd want a front desk where they can enter and exit easily, without anyone seeing them. Where no one can witness them taking Layla in."

"Even if the place has surveillance photos, it wouldn't come until way too late," she added. "You can look up motels online once we're in range. I can think of a few off the top of my head. They'll want something that they could go in and out of quickly, without getting tangled up on side streets. Something near Highway 80."

She sped along the road, heading for the highway entrance.

"Do you think that man will make it off the mountain?" she asked after a while.

"Hard to say. Maybe, with a few scratches. But he knows where your cabin is, and if he knows how to hot-wire your sister's truck, he can drive himself to the hospital."

"Good." Paige didn't realize just how much she needed to hear that there was a way, that the man had a chance. "I heard what you said back on the mountain. About taking someone's life. It sounded like you've thought about that a lot."

Martin glanced over at her and nodded, but it took a moment for him to speak.

"When I started working for my uncle, he wanted me to get a gun. Standard procedure, he said. But you heard my father's position on it, so I had never thought about owning one." He frowned. "Growing up without a gun, I hadn't really considered that idea in the world, what it might mean, so I did a lot of thinking about it. Would I kill someone with it? Maybe people who grow up with them never even really consider this question. They just think it's there for protection. I wondered if people who grow up around guns ever think about the line between protection and aggression. How does carrying a gun influence the other person?"

Martin gave an unexpected laugh. "My uncle told me I was thinking too much about this.

"All he cared about was that I was *protected* when I was working."

"What conclusion did you come to?" she asked. "What does it mean to take someone's life?"

"Probably people don't logically and levelheadedly enter a situation thinking, *I'm going take someone's life.* That's straight up murder. But I think situations quickly escalate, and self-defense can quickly turn into aggression. I never want that to happen to me," he said. "So I made that deal with myself. If I was going to get a gun, I would never kill someone with it."

She felt a warm surge of something that was much more than affection. She had remembered joking, upbeat Martin, but this side had always been there, too—thoughtful, articulate and full of compassion for others. The world hardened that part of too many people, but that hadn't happened to him. He was still the same person, deep down. And though he had said the world had gotten him down, she was grateful it hadn't robbed him of this part of him, the part she loved the very best.

Loved. The word echoed inside her. She swallowed. All the feelings she had before, and seeing the person he was now, had her feeling something more for him. And she could sense the idea taking hold of her with certainty, with the knowledge that she couldn't deny. Love. That's what this was.

Maybe he would go back to his life in San Francisco, and maybe, if she told him how she felt, it would be awkward every time he wandered into town, but she right now, she didn't care. Paige felt her love for Martin flowing through her. She wanted the person next to her, the teenager she'd known on the slopes, so carefree and in charge, so determined to do the right thing, and this man who had faced the world with that same attitude. He had talked about how life had been difficult, but ultimately he hadn't been defeated. Because right now, he was by her side, trying to do the right thing, despite every indication that it might not be possible, that he might fail. She loved him. And she should tell him.

But before Paige could say anything, Martin's voice brought her back to the present.

"I have a cell phone signal."

FOURTEEN

"Thanks," said the officer over the phone line. "I'll trace this plate, and we'll send a squad out to look at the motels, but we don't have much to go on."

"Keep us updated," said Martin. He didn't add that they would be looking for the men, too. As soon as they'd reached cell service, Martin had called the local police and explained the night's events. He'd also provided them with the van's license plate. But that didn't mean the search had ended for him and Paige. They still had a shot at finding Layla before it was too late. Over the years, he'd learned that police didn't like anyone else getting involved with an investigation, mostly for good reasons, such as the dangers of vigilante justice. But Martin had also found that it too often took outside forces to push the department into true investigative mode. On the positive side, at least Mike was now taking Layla's abduction seriously.

After driving past two motels, he was less optimistic. The car had fallen silent. Martin was pretty sure Paige's worries were closing in, and the last thing he wanted to do was feed it. He wasn't willing to think about what happened if every motel in the area turned up nothing. And he really needed to get his gunshot looked at soon.

He tried to stay positive as they turned off the highway

by Donner Pass. The exit served the local ski resort and the national forest, with its forest trails, but early spring was off-season for both skiing and hiking. Few people would be here, if any. The trees were taller in this area, a vast spread of national forest preserved over generations, allowing the forest to grow, the trees feeding each other with their roots, keeping the whole network healthy and strong. There wasn't much in the way of amenities in the area, just a gas station, a ski resort closed for the season with a few patches of melting snow on the slopes, and a motel. They came to a stop and turned left, until two dark brown buildings peeked out of the woods. As they slowed in front of it, Martin's heart sped up. It was isolated, with parking that ran between the two-story buildings and ended in the woods, and only three cars were parked there.

"If I were trying to avoid notice, this is the place I'd choose," he said softly.

"Me, too," said Paige.

He heard that hitch of hope in her voice, and the defeat of the last few minutes was making way for something new. Paige turned off the narrow street, and the motel came into sight. As they approached the driveway, she turned off the headlights, leaving them with the flash of lights from the freeway and the foggy darkness. Martin's heart kicked up into alert.

The motel's two-story buildings seemed to float in the mist. They were long and covered with wooden shingles, and they butted up against the forest. In the mostly empty parking lot there was a white sedan parked in the first space, where the office sign hung, and farther down at the other end of the lot were two more parked vehicles. One was a slick black SUV and behind it there was the glimmer of the silver tail of a truck next to it.

"It's them," said Paige.

"I hope so." He felt that same certainty, but they needed more evidence. There were hundreds of silver trucks around here, and they hadn't looked closely at the make and model of the one when they had driven past this morning. Paige stopped the car in the road, just before the turn-in to the parking lot, and turned off the engine. "What do we do?"

"I think it's time to call the police again," he said.

She closed her eyes. "And say we've found a silver truck? Remember what he said last time? I felt like he just patted me on the head and sent me away."

Martin let out a sigh. "I don't know if it will work, but we should probably try. Before, these men could deny they were involved in this mess, but right now, if we're right, then your sister is being held in one of these rooms. That's something concrete for the police to go on."

Paige swallowed visibly, and a wave of sympathy washed over him. He worked with people disappointed with police efforts all the time. It was why his uncle's business thrived. Maybe it was because, in some cases, the police didn't do everything they could, and sometimes they did the wrong thing. But more often, it was because people expected far too much. Not every situation should be solved by the police. They weren't social workers, they weren't counselors, and they had so few tools to deal with the problems they confronted.

Martin had had plenty of these thoughts over the years, and plenty of ideas for answers—answers that involved better support on everything from addiction to domestic abuse. But right now, none of that mattered. Right now, the most important thing was that they used all the resources they had to save Layla. And that meant trying to get the police to help, even if Paige didn't think it would be successful.

He tried again. "Let me make a call. I'm not sure it will help in this case, but I think there's a chance it will. So let's try."

Paige opened her eyes and turned to him, and her face was full of so many emotions. He could see she was trying to rein them in, and if the time came, he was sure she could. But right now, she looked vulnerable. He laid his hand on the console between them, face up, an invitation for comfort. She looked down at it, her gaze soft, and then she took her hand off the wheel and placed it in his. Warm. Her hand was small and yet strong, and she squeezed his gently. "Thank you."

There was something in the way she spoke, in the way she said his name and the way she looked at him that made his chest feel like it was expanding, like he could breathe easier, like she was filling him with air—air he hadn't realize he needed until this moment.

This was love. He couldn't turn away from it any longer.

"I'm here for you, Paige," he started. "Now and whenever you need it. I promise."

He let go of her hand and took her phone again to dial the police. Nothing happened. He tried again. Nothing. He stared at the screen. "We're out of range again."

"Maybe that's another reason they'd choose this motel."

They couldn't call for help.

"I'm not leaving," she added flatly.

It was, in fact, exactly what he thought they should do.

"Then we wait," he said. He shifted in his seat and winced. The gunshot was sapping his energy. "Unless we want to drive just a little and find service…"

"No." The word sounded final, and he could hear from her voice that she wouldn't compromise on that. "I'm not leaving my sister here."

The car was silent.

"Then we watch," he finally said. "And figure out our next move."

Martin turned to Paige, and she had a faraway look in her eyes. "She's close," Paige whispered. "This has to be the place. I can feel it."

He couldn't pretend to understand this twin instinct, but it hadn't led them astray so far today. Paige leaned forward in her seat, peering around the car next to them, down the dark row of motel room doors.

Martin tried to ignore the increasing ache in his shoulder and focus. "They'd want a first-floor room. Easier in and out."

"Those three rooms at the end, where the cars are parked," she said, pointing. "It has to be one of those."

He nodded.

"There's a second car. If I run down there, I can get a picture of both license plates," she said. "They're meeting someone here, so all of them will be in the same place."

Paige rested her hand on the door handle, and he could see the nervous excitement on her face.

"No." Martin said it a little louder than he meant to. He really wished he hadn't been shot, and it had nothing to do with the burning sensation in his shoulder. He couldn't let her go out there alone. "Let's park across from the rooms. And watch first."

Paige closed her eyes and nodded. She put the car into gear, and they slowly moved forward into the parking lot. She pulled into the space across from the silver truck.

"Now we can—" His words faded at he saw movement. The shift in the curtain was so small that he had almost missed it, but it was there. "I saw something. On the bottom floor, room 113."

Paige sat up in her seat, but the curtain was hanging straight again.

"They might not know what our truck looks like since we parked farther down the road, so let's hope we can stay under their radar," she said as she strained in her seat, trying to get a glimpse.

"If they come out with Layla, all we can do is follow," he said firmly.

"I know," she said in a voice that suggested her mind knew but her heart hadn't quite gotten there yet.

Martin shifted for a better view of the room behind them, but the pain in his shoulder was getting worse.

Paige craned in her seat. "I can't see the license plate."

He tried to turn again, but stars crept into his vision as the burning sensation in his shoulder took over. Paige took off her seat belt and climbed over the console and into the back seat, then took out her phone, likely zooming in on the license plate.

"I still don't have a good shot," she said. "I need to get closer."

"No," he said firmly.

She frowned at him.

"Sorry," he said, "but I don't like that idea. They could come out at any time."

"Let me get these photos, and then we can leave and find reception."

And then they could let the police handle the rest. He wanted so much to believe that this plan would work, that the police could help Layla get free. That a police car wouldn't escalate the situation. He had to believe that because he wasn't going to make it much longer.

"If there's any movement, you need to come back. Right

away," he said, and he could hear the urgency in his voice, the demand, so he added, *"Please."*

She nodded. "I will."

Still, his stomach dropped as she climbed out the driver's side of the truck and into the dark night. She was so vulnerable as she crept through the darkness, crossing the small parking lot quickly and squatting in front of the silver truck. Then she pulled out her phone. He watched her wipe the mud off the license plate with her fingers. He wanted to keep his eyes on her, to make sure she was all right, but he forced himself to check the window where he'd seen movement.

The rain had finally let up, but the fog was thick and ghostly, blowing, winding in tendrils. Was Layla behind the door to room 113, or was their best guess wrong? He glanced again at Paige, who was now leaning over the windshield of the oversize black SUV, getting a shot of the VIN number.

When he looked back at room 113, he froze. Because someone had just opened the door, and he was looking straight at her.

Paige's heart exploded in her chest. Logically, she knew she should run straight back to the car, but her feet wouldn't move. All she could do was stare at the door. Was Layla inside? Was she okay? She held her breath, waiting, paralyzed by layers of fear as the man started for her.

"Paige."

Martin's low voice shot through the night, startling her out of her daze. She turned to the car, the shadow of Martin's face barely there through the dark windshield. Martin, who had been shot. Who was waiting for her to get back into the car. She had to move.

"The twin," shouted the man. "She's out here."

Paige glanced back at the doorway. The heavyset man was running toward her, and just behind her in the doorway she caught a glimpse of Layla's red jacket, but her face was obscured.

"Layla!" she screamed.

The figure in the jacket froze. Another man sprinted out the doorway, followed by the tall man, brandishing a gun. Paige turned, running for three steps, then changed directions, zigzagging. The gun went off, an ear-splitting boom, followed by glass shattering. Martin's windshield? Paige went numb with panic as she sprinted toward the SUV. Where did it hit? The worst-case scenario ran through her mind as she zigged and zagged toward the vehicle. Her heart pulled between two people she loved—*loved*—and right now, it felt like it had finally ripped. What if she lost them both?

Paige tore open the door and another deafening shot rang out. There was a pop, the hiss of air. They'd hit the tire, from the sound of it. But Martin was in front of her, pulling her into the driver's seat with his uninjured arm. And there, lodged into the metal frame of the seat, was a bullet. She met Martin's gaze, her heart exploding again with fear. If she had been sitting there or if he had been driving…

"Thank the Lord you're safe," she choked out as she crouched into the seat, fumbling with the keys. The engine roared to life, and she looked out through the spiderweb of cracks on the windshield. A blur of red flashed in the darkness, heading for the forest. *Layla.*

She'd gotten away.

Paige needed to follow her sister…but Martin was next to her with a bullet wound in his arm.

"Follow her," he said, as if he could read her mind. "The tires run on flats. We can do it."

She threw the car into Drive and squinted through the ruined glass, driving toward the dark woods. Lights flashed as the silver truck's engine roared, but she focused on the red coat, barely visible in the darkness.

The misty clouds glowed, obscuring her vision through the windshield as they jolted over the curb of the parking lot and into the forest. Layla's coat was getting closer, and she saw a glimpse of something silver, but headlights glared in the rearview mirror. The men were close behind.

"I counted two men running after her on foot," said Martin over his shoulder as he craned his neck out the window.

Paige wove the car through the trees, bumping over stumps and fallen branches. They were close, so close. She saw her twin appear just ahead.

"Layla!" she shouted out the window. "Get in."

Layla turned, then doubled back as Paige swung around, putting the car between the men on foot and Layla. Martin unlocked the door, and Layla dove into the back seat, holding her laptop to her chest.

"I know who it is," gasped Layla. "I'm almost sure of it."

"That only matters if we get out of here," said Paige.

She slammed the gear into Reverse, turning the car to face the silver truck as her sister fumbled with her seat belt. In the distance, she saw the flash of red and blue lights, but the headlights from their pursuers still blinded her. The truck wasn't slowing down. It was coming right at them.

"Brace yourself," yelled Martin, and he reached for Paige's hand.

But before she touched his fingers, the front of their car was hit in a sickening crunch. Paige jolted forward in her seat. Then everything went black.

FIFTEEN

Martin opened his eyes. He was in a hospital bed, there was an IV tube sticking out of his arm. He looked around the sterile, beige room. A trickle of hospital professionals passed outside the room on their way to somewhere else. He looked from one side to the other as a panic welled up in him once again. He shifted in his bed, trying to sit up, but his arm protested.

"Hello?" he called to an attendant in yellow scrubs passing by.

The man entered the room. "Mr. Hosey? How are you feeling?"

"I'll live," he said with a wince as he pulled himself to sit. "But where is Paige Addison?"

The man frowned and shook his head. "Unfortunately, I can't give you information about other patients." Then his expression softened. "You were brought in the same ambulance with her, but you're not listed as a relation."

His pounding heart sped up, and the dizziness from before was starting to take over. He forced himself to calm down. He would do her no good like this.

"Is she alive?"

The man looked around, then gave him the slightest of nods.

Thank you, Lord.

"I want to see her. That's allowed, right?"

The attendant's gaze was sympathetic. "First we need to check you out, just to make sure that you're okay to be up and moving around before I let you go."

Martin sank back on the bed. "Where are we?"

"Sierra Nevada Memorial Hospital. Grass Valley."

"What time is it?"

"Just after midnight."

So much time had passed. Too much.

"What about Paige's twin, Layla?"

The man frowned. "Only you and one more person were admitted."

Martin closed his eyes and nodded. What had happened to Layla? He endured the poking and prodding. Lights were shone in his eyes, as he looked one way and the other, praying for patience.

He looked over at the pole next to him. "I have an IV?"

"Antibiotics. That gunshot is no joke. It was bleeding for a while, and it needed more than a few pads of gauze." The man's voice held a hint of rebuke, as if he knew Martin had chosen not to seek help immediately.

"That was a temporary fix," he muttered. "There were other things we had to take care of first."

Except he had no idea if they'd taken care of those other things. He fought the growing impatience as he answered each one of the hospital staff's questions, showing that he wasn't suffering from memory loss. Yes, he remembered everything. Not just the date and the president and all their other questions. He also remembered every moment of the day before, every fearful threat, every setback. And then he was thinking of Paige. What it felt like to be next to her, together again, so like their past and yet so different. And each time he thought of her, he was struck by a pang of helplessness. He needed to see Paige and Layla and make sure they were okay.

It was his grandmother's voice that rang in his ears, his grandmother who had welcomed him into her home every Sunday, even when he hadn't shown up for church, even when he only muttered a couple words all meal. She always hugged him and harassed him about whether he was eating and sleeping enough. She always showed her love for him, her insightful attention as to exactly what was going on with him. And though it made him squirm, he had come back every Sunday because, he knew, somewhere deep down, she was right. He wasn't in control.

He needed to accept that. Even if it meant accepting the heartache that this world seemed determined to give him. *Give yourself over to the Lord.*

Somehow, he made it through the doctor's exam, and somehow, with a reluctant nod, she said, "I'm not ready to discharge you, but if you can walk, you might want to make a visit to room number seven, down the hall."

Martin, dressed in a pair of scrubs lent to him and in his stocking feet, rolled his IV down the hall with his wounded arm in a sling, knowing he looked as vulnerable as he felt.

The door to room number seven was open and his stomach dropped as he saw Paige. Her arm was in a cast, and her eyes were closed. She was hooked up to all sorts of monitors that sounded their slow steady beats. The doctor had suggested she was alive, though that was cold comfort because she clearly wasn't out of the woods yet. She wasn't awake. So he pulled up a bland wooden chair next to the bed with his uninjured arm and he sat down on it. He took her hand in his, remembering her strong grip, the tenacity of her hold despite all the fears. They had been there for each other all day. But now her hand was limp. He would need to do the holding now. He would need to be the strong one.

He had promised himself that he'd tell her how he felt when they were out of this mess, and the urgency of that promise weighed on him. But there was nothing he could do about it right now, so he bowed his head, concentrating on her warm hand in his, and he prayed.

Paige woke up feeling out of sorts, surrounded by strange sounds and scents. She wanted to open her eyes, but her eyelids felt so heavy. Where was she? The question was startling, but immediately, before fear could take hold, she was aware of her hand. It was fitted into another one, so warm and familiar and strong.

Martin's hand. She knew it at once, without opening her eyes. It was the hand that had steadied her through the day, reminded her to hope, buoyed her. It had been strong when she was fading. And now he was here by her side. Paige took a breath. Another. Then, slowly, she forced her eyes open.

Martin sat on a chair next to her bed. His head was bent and his eyes were closed. His lips were moving slightly. She took a breath, trying not to move, just so she had the chance to take him in. He was so strong. She studied his neat haircut, his warm brown skin, his broad shoulders, bandaged, resilient. He was here to support her, even now. More memories from the day threatened, thunderous, but Martin was here, and she focused on that. She squeezed his hand, and he sat at alert, his eyes wide.

"Paige," he whispered, like she was God's miracle, just for him, especially delivered for him.

Her heart burst with warmth and overwhelming feelings brimmed through her. "You're here."

The words were choked in her throat, and she gave a little cough, the dryness. He let go of her hand and reached for a cup of water on the bedside table.

She lifted her hand to take the cup from him, but it felt heavy, shaky.

"Can I help you with this?" he asked.

She nodded.

He slipped his hand behind her head with infinite tenderness, lifted her slightly, then brought the cup to her mouth. She swallowed. The liquid trailed through her body, rejuvenating, helping everything come into focus.

The pieces of the day came back in all their chaos, and at the center was her sister. Where was she?

"Is there news about Layla?" she whispered.

"I'll go ask the staff if she was here." Martin disappeared, then returned a few moments later. "The receptionist said someone who looked like you was here not long ago."

Paige closed her eyes. Her sister was alive. Thank God.

"I'll figure out where she is," said Martin, like he wore the weight of the world on his shoulders, like he held himself responsible. "But I came here first."

"As long as I know she's alive," she said quietly, looking at him again. He was so handsome, his warm brown skin, his high cheekbones, his dark eyes so full of compassion. Her stomach fluttered. They had been through so much, and she needed tell him how she felt. Paige bit her lip, then told herself she'd work her way up to it. "How's your shoulder?"

"I'll need some time off for healing, but the doctor says I should be able to fully recover soon."

She quietly took that in. "What does that mean for your job?"

"The upside is that my parents will be happy. I'll probably stay with them and take it easy for a while."

Regret surged through her, regret that she had brought this on Martin. But he was gazing at her with a look that was so far from recrimination. The warmth in his eyes took her breath away. She wanted to come clean about how she felt, even if it meant facing rejection once again. As soon as she found the right moment. Martin squeezed her hand, and she closed her eyes and let the inner calm come back to her, the calm that she found even when circumstances were difficult, desperate.

"I really wish you hadn't gotten shot over this," she said quietly.

"I chose this path, Paige. I'm in it to protect anyone who is a target. And I accept the risk that comes with it."

She gave him a little smile. "I get it. I guess I just wish that you didn't actually have to make the sacrifice."

"That's exactly what I was thinking when I walked into your hospital room."

He held her gaze, and it felt as if their past and their present were coming together, lighting a path for a future. In that moment, Paige knew she had to say what was on her mind, the feeling that had grown inside her since yesterday. She could feel how close they came to missing this chance. She wasn't going to let it get away.

"I care about you," she blurted out, then her face heated with embarrassment. "I mean, not just as a friend. As more."

Paige bit her lip. She really could have done that a little more smoothly. Martin blinked at her in surprise.

She forced herself to continue. "You don't have to say anything. It's just that I promised myself that when this was over, I would tell you that I think you are the most wonderful man. Maybe I was even a little in love with you in high school, but this is different. I—"

She broke off into another coughing fit, which seemed to startle Martin into action. He lifted the cup for another drink of water, and she took another sip. He put the cup back on the bedside table, then he leaned forward and pressed his lips against her forehead. The kiss was so tender and gentle it took her breath away. But doubt flooded through her. Did he feel the same, or was this simply consolation? But when his brown eyes met hers, they were filled with openness, with a kind of affection that made her heart feel like it was going to burst. Then his mouth hitched up in the hint of a smile.

"I promised myself that when you woke up, I'd tell you that I was in love with you. I promised I would tell you how much I admire you, how much I want with all my heart what is best for you." He let out a little laugh. "I guess you beat me to it."

She felt something bubbling up in her. Despite her worries about her sister, she was smiling. This was more than just happiness. It was something inside, telling her on the deepest level that this was right. This man had always been right for her, both the boy she had known and cared for as a friend and the man he was now, whom she loved. This was the person who was right for her. This was whom she wanted.

He leaned forward and he pressed his lips to hers. The kiss was soft and full of understanding of who they once were and who they were now. In the kiss, she could feel that he knew her, fully, and he loved every part of her. That he would be there for her, even through the toughest times. She could feel that this would be forever.

He pulled back and stared, as if he was taking everything in, too.

Thank you, Lord. You give me strength when my own is at its end. I wouldn't have that alone, not without You, not without Martin, not without my sister... Her sister wasn't there, but if she could get a hold of a phone…

"I need to try to call Layla," she said, then turned to the phone next to her bedside. "Do you know how to use this thing?"

"I'll figure it out." He handed her the receiver, then studied the instructions on the face of the beige face of the phone. He pushed a couple buttons until she heard a dial tone. Paige reached over to dial her sister's number.

Her breath caught in her throat when she heard her sister's voice. "Layla?"

"Paige." Her sister's voice came through after the first ring. "I'm in the lobby. I'll be right there."

A few minutes later, there was movement in the doorway. When she glanced up, Layla was walking toward her. Her sister was wearing the same clothes she'd been wearing in the back of the van, and she looked like she hadn't slept, but the expression on her face was elated. Paige understood those feelings perfectly.

Her sister rushed to the bedside and threw her arms around her, and then she closed her eyes and felt relief, that bone-deep knowledge that they were safe.

"I'm so sorry, Paige," Layla whispered. "I can't believe I got you into this mess. I tried so hard to avoid it, but I didn't know they would come for you."

Paige shook her head. "Don't be sorry."

Layla let go, looked at Martin, then back at her. "The police came. I guess the hotel owner called them, and they weren't far."

"What about your story?" Paige asked.

"I finished it in the waiting room, and I think it's online already," said Layla, taking her phone out of her pocket. She typed and scrolled, then handed her phone to Paige. Paige motioned for Martin to come closer, and he settled gently next to her on the bed, looking over her shoulder.

Nevada Hotel Family Implicated in Illegal Mining Scheme

Bribery. Kidnapping. Illegal mining. These are just three of the alleged crimes of five members of the once-prominent Cooper family, led by disgraced Nevada hotel magnet Gerard "Boss" Cooper. He has been charged with felony counts of interstate kidnapping in an operation that involved both California and Nevada police. But what lay behind this was a quiet operation that all points back to the rare-mineral mining industry exploding across the world...

"Boss," she whispered to Martin. "The boss they kept mentioning…"

He nodded. "I thought they meant *their* boss, but they were talking about Cooper. They were all family."

Paige nodded. "Which was why those men looked so much alike."

Layla shook her head. "I can't believe you two got mixed up in this."

"You're making a calculation that it's worth the risk, Layla," Paige said. "Let me make it, too."

"Same," added Martin, resting his hand on Paige's shoulder, filling her with warmth.

Layla let out a long sigh. "Now that I can see we're all

going to be okay, I can say it was actually good that all of this happened. Otherwise, Gerard Cooper would still be out there, with only the accusations. But the kidnapping made the threat imminent. So, strangely, it's what protects us."

Paige was grateful for that. Because everything that had happened brought them to this point.

Layla rounded the bed and gave Martin a hug. Then Layla straightened and raised her eyebrows. She waved her finger from Martin to Paige and back again. "Is this a thing?"

Martin laid his hand on Paige's, and she laced her fingers with his.

"It is," she said.

"Good," said her sister. "Finally. I always thought you two would be perfect together." Martin gave a little snort of laughter. "You should have mentioned that earlier."

He squeezed Paige's hand, and her heart soared. She was sitting with her sister and the man she was in love with, and they were all safe here next to her. Hope blossomed inside her, and for that, she was grateful.

EPILOGUE

One year later...

Paige stomped off her ski boots on the concrete staircase outside the mountaintop restaurant, then walked across the rubber mats and through the heavy wooden doors, brushing wispy flakes of snow off her jacket. Another set of glass doors opened into the heart of the building. She pulled off her gloves and goggles and scanned the long tables, searching for a spot next to the tall windows that looked out onto the snow-covered peaks.

And then she spotted his red ski patrol jacket in the crowd. He'd found an empty table in the corner, and in front of him were two large cups, hopefully hot chocolate. Paige's heart sped up as she crossed the room, her ski boots clomping over the wet floor. Martin looked so handsome, with his ski cap pulled over the short cut of his hair, his coat unzipped and brown eyes sparkling. He broke into a smile when he saw her, that wide grin she remembered from all those years ago, joy with the tiniest hint of mischief. That grin had been slow to come back, but as he'd recovered at his parents' place during the summer, she'd seen it more and more. After he'd sold his apartment in San Francisco and bought a little house just off Main Street in Clover Valley, walking distance from Hosey's Outdoor Adventure Sports, he flashed that smile regularly for her.

In the months that followed what Paige hoped was the most frightening day of her life, the Cooper family's complicated scheme was slowly unearthed. They'd bought up low-price land and sold shares promising rare-mineral metal markets lucrative electric batteries. This scheme meant hiring undocumented workers, taking advantage of their vulnerable position to keep them quiet. Many times, Paige had thought of the people who had come to this country, hoping to find a way for their families to survive, only to get caught in this illegal ordeal. Paige was so proud of the work that her sister had done to uncover this. Her story had helped stop the illegal mining and shone a light on the terrible conditions and unfair practices the workers faced. Arrests had been made and trials were set to begin soon. Paige prayed for justice.

Her sister had gotten a lot of recognition for her work and had even gotten an offer for a job at *The LA Times*. But much to Paige's surprise, Layla had turned it down in favor of staying closer to Paige. Paige had then convinced her sister that they should take a week off every now and then to spend time at their grandmother's cabin together, just the two of them…and Maggie, of course.

Martin still did some work for his uncle's private investigation firm, but more often he'd been working at the family store again. And now that winter had descended, he was getting his skiing back to top form. He was in transition, trying to decide what he wanted next. Paige hoped the life he decided on involved her, too. She'd made that conclusion last summer, that this was the man she wanted to be with forever, but he had been through enough changes these last months that she'd held off saying those words directly.

Maybe soon. She'd floated the idea of asking him to marry her, but her mother, who had always been more traditional, insisted she give him time.

"He'll ask you soon enough," her mom said. "I know he will."

So she'd done her best to be patient…at least for a little longer. If he didn't ask her by next summer, she was going to take matters into her own hands. After all, it was also her mother who had once told her that if she wanted something badly enough, she needed to go for it.

She slid into the chair across from him and laid her gloves and goggles on the table.

"How was your afternoon?" he asked, sliding a cup of hot chocolate in front of her. "I heard the call over the radio."

"A little intense," she said. "A guy went off a jump and broke his leg, so he was in a lot of pain, and his daughter was really scared."

"Good thing you had that junior patroller on your team," he said with a hint of a smile.

"They're the best."

"Definitely."

She chuckled, thinking back to their own adventures. "She did great, talking to the daughter, listening to her story and comforting her while I triaged and got the guy onto the sled."

"I'm sure you all were fantastic."

During the fall, Paige had started the EMT program at the local community college. While she liked her work as a home health care worker and loved the one-on-one care she could give people in need, reuniting with Martin had reopened the part of her that liked adventure, even thrived on it. She'd thought this part of her had gone away. It had been such a long time since she'd felt it, but after what she, Layla and Martin had gone through the previous spring, her drive to be useful in an emergency, helping people, had come back. Training new junior ski patrol candidates was her current outlet for it, but she was considering trying other paths, too. Martin had hinted that he'd love her to join his ski patrol team, too, or maybe lead some adventure tours for his parents' store.

"We were on the other side when the call came in," said Martin. "I could hear you had it under control."

Her old internal reflexes kicked in. "I was a little overwhelmed when I saw his daughter so upset."

"But you did it." Martin reached his hand across the table and she intertwined her fingers with his.

"I did."

They'd had conversations about this over the last year, about the confidence she'd slowly had to build most of her life. She'd thought of herself as the less adventurous twin, but Martin had pressed her to rethink that idea. She didn't only exist in comparison with Layla. She had worked on remembering that her bold and adventurous side didn't come from the lack of fear but, rather, the ability to make peace with it, to work with it. And so she had grown, come out of her shell, as Layla put it. Somehow, this had also brought her sister closer, too.

"Early dinner tonight?" he asked. "I'm starving."

"Maybe we just pick up pizza?"

"Or see what my father is making tonight?" He waggled his eyebrows.

Paige laughed. "If he's not tired of making meals for us yet."

"Are you kidding? He's just thrilled I'm back in Clover Valley." Martin winked. "And that I've reconnected with you."

Paige blushed as his eyes softened. Whatever was on his mind, it could wait because she was starving, too.

She squeezed his hand and let go. "I'm going to get some fries to hold us over until we get to your parents' place."

Martin watched Paige walk away, her long brown ponytail swinging, as a mix of excitement and nervousness ran through him. Should he do it today? His parents had given him an antique family ring and their blessing weeks ago, and he knew he wanted to ask Paige to be his wife, but he'd been searching for the right time to ask. Something about this afternoon felt so right, and suddenly he couldn't wait.

Except he hadn't brought the ring with him to the slopes. He had imagined doing this differently: somewhere more private, both of them dressed up and him on one knee, offering the ring from his great-grandmother. It was a lovely idea, and yet something more urgent was calling to him. Maybe it wasn't the perfect setup that mattered. Right now, his heart was thumping and it felt like his chest wasn't big enough to contain it. Maybe this feeling he had was more important than the circumstances. He knew this was true.

They were somewhere special: the ski resort where their friendship had begun, twelve years ago.

Maybe she would want the ceremony at the Clover Valley Church, where she went—or would she be open to a wedding at Taylor Memorial United Methodist Church, where his grandmother and half his family belonged, the church he'd attended when he'd lived in San Francisco? He and Paige had gone to services there together, once with his parents and a few times just the two of them. At first, he wasn't sure how she'd feel about a Black church, but at family dinner at his grandmother's old Victorian house after her first service, she'd talked about how magical it had felt when she walked into the building, with its stained glass and beautiful wooden architecture.

"The place is truly blessed," she'd said, and the whole table had responded with amens.

The next time they'd attended, Paige had taken an apple pie made from her own grandmother's recipe, and his uncle had taken her side and thanked her for the happiness he had seen in Martin since that stressful time back in the spring. His family had embraced her, embraced them both.

Paige was making her way back across the large room, carrying a large plate of fries on a red tray, which she'd picked up at the counter. The afternoon sun shone through the window, making her hair shine, and her smile was so lovely it made Martin's chest ache. Yes, now was the right time.

She slid into the chair across from him. "I ordered a large so you wouldn't eat them all."

"Me?" He gave her an I-have-no-idea-what-you're-talking-about look, and she snorted.

"Yes, you." She picked up a fry and dipped it in the little paper cup of ketchup on the tray. He simply watched.

She rolled her eyes. "You know I was kidding."

He nodded.

"So what are you waiting for?"

He swallowed, then took her hand. They had held hands so many times, as friends, as coworkers, as partners, and every time it felt right.

"What's going on?" she asked, a little wary. "Is something wrong?"

He shook his head. Swallowed again. "Paige, will you marry me?"

She blinked at him, like this was the last thing she thought he'd say.

"Yes," she said softly. "Yes, yes, yes, I'll marry you."

His heart took off, and his chest felt like it was going to burst. Paige stood up, keeping hold of his hand, and he stood up, too. With his other hand, he caressed her flushed cheek with all the hope and tenderness he felt. Then he leaned over and pressed his lips to hers. He could feel his dreams grow, intertwining with hers, becoming something more.

* * * * *

Dear Reader,

Last summer, my son and I took a cross-country trip from California to Michigan. On the very last night, we found the lovely Angel Creek Campground on national forest land in northeast Nevada. The little place was perched on the side of the mountain, with snow-covered peaks on one side, the red-orange desert valley on the other, and cows roaming through the grassy hillside. We set up our tent, and as I lay on my sleeping bag, looking out of the mesh top at the blue sky above, I thought, *This is perfect.*

A few hours later, I wasn't as enthusiastic. First came the lightning, then thunder, then wind and finally rain. Our tent fly came loose, and our stakes were yanked from the ground as gusts of wind whipped down the mountainside. For an hour, my son and I stood inside the tent, holding it up, clinging to the fly from the inside as thunder boomed constantly. At that point, I didn't care if we got wet. I was just praying we didn't get struck by lightning.

Days later, I sat in the comfort of my home, writing about Martin and Paige's own adventures in a mountain storm. I found myself thinking about that last night of our road trip and how easy it can be to forget just how dangerous storms can be until we find ourselves unexpectedly exposed. Martin and Paige have plenty of experience on the mountain, yet they find themselves in unexpected danger, at the mercy of the elements. However—and most importantly—they have each other.

I hope you love their story!
Rebecca